P9-CDJ-672

MYSTERY
AT DEER HILL
BY VIRGINIA FRANCES VOIGHT

SBS SCHOLASTIC BOOK SERVICES
New York • London • Richmond Hill, Ontario

Another book by the Author

THE MISSING $10,000 BILL

This book, in a much abbreviated version, was published in serial form in *The American Girl* magazine under the title "Fawn Island," issues dated January through June, 1957.

6th printing .... October 1967

Printed in the U.S.A.

CONTENTS

To my dear friends,
Anna and Mata Hansen

1. A LETTER FROM MAINE

IT WAS THE FIRST DAY of summer vacation. April Merriman and her chum, Jean Turner, were returning home after an exhilarating morning of shopping. Laden with boxes and packages, they left the bus at Ivy Lane and lingered on the corner to talk about the things they had bought: bathing suits, shorts, blouses, play shoes, and gay cottons to be made up into whirling skirts. All had been purchased in happy anticipation of a summer at the beach.

April was in an especially vivacious mood because this was the first time her mother had allowed her to do important shopping on her own. She had enjoyed every moment of the long morning. It had even been fun trying to stretch her clothes allowance to cover all the extras she longed for, but could not afford.

April and Jean had been friends since grammar school days, and now their freshman year at Hartford High was behind them. During summer vacations they lived in neighboring cottages in a crowded Connecticut summer colony on Long Island Sound. The cottages were built even closer together than houses in a city, but the sandy beach curved smooth and golden before them, with rocks jutting up at each end of the crescent to give a breezy privacy to the little group of cottages. Everyone knew everyone else, and the same families had been coming every summer for years and years.

April loved the familiar safeness of Crescent Beach, the snug old cottage with its wide veranda, and the dancing waters of the Sound stretching away to the hazy blue line of Long Island on the horizon. She could not imagine a summer without the swimming, and the long hours of sunning herself on the beach in the company of her friends; the boating and beach parties; and the dances for young people Saturday nights in the gray, weathered Roller Skating Rink at the Point, with Mom and Daddy, or some other parents, for chaperones.

"When is your family moving to the beach, April?" Jean asked.

April sighed. "Not until after the Fourth. Daddy's

vacation begins the second week in July. He likes to get us settled at Crescent Beach and spend the first weeks with us, before he starts coming down for just week ends."

Suddenly April remembered that it was Thursday, the day her mother spent with the Church Sewing Circle. April was supposed to get lunch for herself and her brother, Perry.

"I'll see you tomorrow afternoon, Jean," she said hastily. "Don't forget to bring your skirt pattern when you come over."

Jean nodded and waved in a gesture of farewell.

April hurried along the sidewalk to the Merriman house at the corner of a block of comfortable-looking homes, well kept lawns, and gardens where roses and irises flung out the exquisite colors of June.

Perry Merriman, who liked to josh his sister about her fastidiousness, sometimes called her "a lace petticoat girl." April rather enjoyed being thought of in that way. Because of her medium height and the fact that she was just slightly on the plump side, she felt that she must take special pains with her grooming. Slim little Jean could take chances with a casualness that sometimes bordered on sloppiness. Not April! Today, after the arduous morning in the shops, she still looked as fresh and dainty as when she had left home. The full skirt of her red-and-white checked gingham dress swung crisply over her flounced, polished cotton petticoat; her white

3

Eton jacket set beautifully; and the red ribbon that tied her dark brown hair into a pony tail still had its perky look.

Halfway down the block she came to a sudden stop. Sonny Jones was in his front yard, two doors from Merriman's, playing with his new puppy. The taffy-colored spaniel, looking all oversized feet and flying ears, was tearing about in wide circles. Suddenly he spotted April and galloped toward her, wriggling his fat body and wagging his stumpy tail.

"Call your dog, Sonny!" April cried in a tone of panic.

"Aw, for crying out loud, Beans won't hurt you!" the little boy protested.

He ran after the puppy and scooped him up in his arms.

Beans strained toward April, his pink tongue flashing out.

"He wants to kiss you," Sonny laughed.

April stepped around them, giving them a wide berth.

"Don't you let him go until I'm on my porch!" she warned Sonny.

"You'd think Beans was a tiger or something," Sonny grumbled.

Safe on her own porch, April wished with all her heart that there could be a law prohibiting people from keeping dogs in the city. A boisterous, muddy-pawed puppy like Beans was hazard enough, but she felt weak from fear every time she had to pass the boxer that

4

lived with the family next door to Jean, although the boxer never paid her any attention at all, friendly or otherwise.

In spite of a good deal of pleading from Perry, the Merrimans had never had a pet, because Mom was afraid that dogs might bite her children, or cats might scratch them. April mirrored her mother's fear of animals. Unlike Perry, she had never yearned for a pet. Yet there had been times when, from a safe distance, she had watched a friend play with a cat or dog, and wondered whether she might not be missing some richly satisfying experience in not having a pet of her own. But the feeling had always been vague and fleeting.

As April opened the front door, she saw mail on the hall floor where it had been dropped through the slit in the door. She carried her packages to her bedroom and then went back to pick up the letters and magazines. One letter was for her, from her Aunt Ellen, who was vacationing somewhere in the state of Maine. Before April could open it, Perry burst into the house.

A year older than April, and a year ahead of her at Hartford High, he was a happy-natured boy, exploding with energy.

"What's for lunch? I'm starving!"

"You're always starving." April laid the unopened letter on the kitchen table and peered into the refrigerator. "I'll have lunch ready in a jiffy," she promised.

April tied on one of her mother's dainty aprons. She

5

liked to cook and it was fun to work by herself in the shining yellow-and-white kitchen. There were flowered chintz valances over the windows and potted begonias stood on the sills. She made hamburger patties and set them to broil in the electric oven.

Mom always left a special treat for April and Perry on her days out—today it was individual shortcakes of rich biscuit dough, baked and ready to be buttered and reheated. In the refrigerator was a bowl of hulled and sweetened strawberries. April split hamburger buns and sliced tomatoes. Having washed up, Perry put the place mats on the round table by the window and poured tall glasses full of milk.

He noticed the letter at April's place and picked it up to glance at the postmark.

"Bear Paw, Maine," he read aloud. "Aunt Ellen sure picked a primitive-sounding spot for her vacation."

"The doctor told her she needed rest and quiet," April reminded him.

She whisked the sizzling brown hamburgers onto the buns and decorated each one with a slice of tomato. She spooned strawberries over the hot shortcakes and drifted whipped cream over them.

"Mmm," Perry approved, as they slid into their chairs at the table. He sampled his hamburger. "You're almost as good a cook as Mom, Sis." Halfway through his hamburger, he said pensively, "I wish we could spend a vacation in the Maine woods."

April stared at him over the rim of her glass of milk. "You mean you don't want to go to Crescent Beach?"

"Gosh, April, we've been to Crescent Beach every summer since I was eight. Wouldn't you like to see some other part of the country, and get to know someone beside the same old crowd?"

April looked shocked. "The kids at Crescent Beach are our *friends*—we would never have as much fun with new people. I thought you liked the beach as much as I do."

"It's nothing against Crescent Beach or our old pals there to want to see something new," Perry defended. "From the way you always have your nose poked into some travel or adventure book, I should think you'd want to see for yourself what lies beyond Hartford and Crescent Beach. I saw you reading *The Treasure of Yucatan* the other day. If Jim Alder had stuck in one place all his life, books like that and his *Alaskan Snows* would never have been written."

April laughed. "I'm glad that authors like Jim Alder travel to far places and write books about them, so I can have adventures right here at home, where it's safe and comfortable."

Perry attacked his shortcake. "Say, this is the best! The trouble with you," he added, continuing the discussion, "is that Mom has always kept you in a glass case. If the case ever gets broken, you may find out that it's fun to have adventures of your own."

April was reading her letter.

"Aunt Ellen says she is getting a wonderful rest, and she has fallen in love with Maine," she told Perry.

April and Perry were as fond of their young aunt as if she were as close as an older sister.

Ellen Merriman had taken a leave of absence from her job as catalogist at a library to nurse her mother through a serious, long-drawn-out illness. Now Grandma Merriman had been dead a year, and Ellen herself had been ill from nervous exhaustion. She was better now, but the doctor had advised a summer in some quiet spot before she returned to her work at the library. Ellen had answered an attractive-sounding advertisement in the Sunday paper, with the result that she had rented a small cottage in the Maine woods for the summer. She had driven up there two weeks ago and, except for a postcard announcing her safe arrival, April's letter was the first the Merrimans had heard from her.

"'This is beautiful wilderness country,'" April read aloud. "'Tall pines and hemlocks sigh around my cottage, the air is like crystal spring water. It is a lovely walk through the woods to Mik-Chik Pond, but as yet the water is too cold for swimming. Walking home from the farmhouse where my landlord lives, I saw two deer feeding at the edge of the apple orchard, and Kent Oliver, the boy at the farm, saw a moose swimming across Mik-Chik Pond one day last week.'"

April shuddered. She had once seen a moose in a nature movie, a blackish, hulking creature with danger-ous-looking antlers; Aunt Ellen could enjoy having moose for neighbors if she liked, but April wanted none of such brutes or the wild, formidable country where they lived.

The next moment she gave a cry of dismay. "Aunt Ellen wants me to go to Bear Paw and spend the sum-mer with her!"

"She must be lonesome, in spite of the deer and moose," grinned Perry. "But what a lucky break for you, Sis."

April looked at him as though she thought he must be crazy. "I am not going," she said flatly. "Wild horses could not drag me to Bear Paw."

Perry shook his head sadly. "Girls sure are the crazi-est!"

He finished drinking his milk and pushed back his chair.

"You wash and I'll dry," he said to April, as he car-ried his dishes to the sink. "And get a wiggle on! I've still a sizable piece of lawn to mow before I meet Tom John-son at the tennis court."

"Oh, run along," April told him. "I'll do the dishes by myself. I've got to stay here anyhow because Mom asked me to bake a cake for dinner."

"Make it chocolate," Perry said, twitching her pony tail as he passed her on his way to the door.

April made a chocolate layer cake and tidied up the kitchen. Then she went to her room to unwrap her packages and arrange her purchases of the morning on the bed so her mother could see them when she came home. Her eyes sparkled with delight as she held the shirred, strawberry red bathing suit up against her body and looked in the long mirror set into the back of her bedroom door. Imagine wasting this darling suit in the middle of the Maine woods, with no one to see it but wild animals!

Her face sobered. It was going to be difficult to explain to Aunt Ellen why she didn't want to accept her invitation; she'd have to ask Mom to help her write a tactful refusal.

April's mother and father both arrived home at the same time that evening. April had put in the oven the chicken casserole which her mother had prepared that morning. Her mother snatched a moment before supper to whisk into April's room and approve the things she had bought. But they didn't have time really to discuss anything because Perry kept howling from the hall that he was starving, and Daddy put his head inside the bedroom door to say whimsically that whatever was cooking in the oven sure smelled delicious, and when was he going to get a chance to sample it.

"The men in this family are always more concerned with what's to eat than anything else," April laughed, as she helped her mother get the dinner on the table.

After Daddy had said grace, and everyone was served, Mom had news of various church activities to tell the rest of the family, and Daddy had some interesting stories to tell of his day in court. It wasn't until they were leaving the table that April remembered her aunt's letter.

"Oh!" she exclaimed. "I had a letter from Aunt Ellen. I left it on the table in the living room for you and Mom to read, Daddy."

Mr. Merriman had finished reading his sister's letter by the time April and her mother had cleared the table and joined him in the living room. He smiled at April as he handed the letter to his wife.

"Your trip to Maine will be a wonderful experience for you, April."

April stood still in the center of the room, staring at him as he sat in his easy chair.

"But I'm not going to Maine, Daddy."

"Not going! Why not?" her father demanded.

"I wouldn't give up Crescent Beach for anything."

He laughed. "You have plenty of vacations at Crescent Beach ahead of you. The Maine woods will be something new and inspiring. I'll never forget a fishing trip I had in Maine when I was a boy."

"But you went with Grandpa," April protested. "Aunt Ellen expects me to travel to Maine by myself."

"Going alone will give you some much needed self-confidence," her father assured her.

"But Daddy, I'm scared to travel by myself," April burst out.

She glanced appealingly at her mother. Mrs. Merriman was sitting on the sofa with the letter in her hand, listening to the conversation with a troubled expression on her pleasant face.

"I might not get off at the right place," April continued. "I might end up in some place none of us ever heard of before."

Perry glanced up from the chair where he was reading the evening comics.

"We could pin a tag on you," he offered. " 'Please put this little girl off the train at Bear Paw, Maine.' "

April swung around to wrinkle her nose at him.

"Why can't Perry go instead of me?" she asked her father.

"Because your aunt invited you." Mr. Merriman looked at his wife. "Don't you agree with me, Beth, that April should accept Ellen's invitation? The family owes Ellen some consideration after the way she cared for Mother, and because of her own illness."

Mrs. Merriman sighed. A gentle-mannered woman, as exquisite in her person as she had taught April to be, she loved to have her children under her sheltering wing. But she was also deeply attached to her sister-in-law.

"I know you would prefer to go to the beach with us," she told April slowly. "But Aunt Ellen will see to it that you have a good time in Maine. And she would be so disappointed if you refused her invitation."

12

As if that put an end to the discussion, Mr. Merriman walked over to the television set and switched on his favorite news commentator.

"I'm going over to help Tom fix his bike," Perry told his mother.

After Perry had gone, April sat down on the sofa and tucked her hand under her mother's arm.

"Oh Mom, I don't want to go to Maine!" she whispered. "Must I really go?"

Her mother gave her hand a loving squeeze.

"I am afraid your father is set on your going," she said sympathetically. "And you wouldn't want to hurt Ellen. You have always enjoyed going places with her—"

"I wouldn't enjoy going to a place named Bear Paw with *anyone*," April said with a shudder.

Then, because her mother looked so upset, she felt a pang of conscience. Mom was trying to make the best of things, but April knew that in her heart her mother did not like the idea of her going off to Maine for the summer any better than April herself liked it. But if Daddy had made up his mind that she was to go, there was no sense in struggling.

"I guess it will be all right," she murmured to her mother. "Once I get used to the idea."

Her mother smiled in a relieved fashion and patted her hand.

The faces on the television screen blurred to April's

sight. In another moment she was going to start bawling like an infant!

She got hastily to her feet. "I'm going out to the kitchen to call Jean."

In the kitchen, she leaned her head against the wall for a moment, glad that Perry was not here to see the babyish tears that flooded her eyes. Then she swallowed hard to force down the lump in her throat, and dialed Jean's number on the wall telephone. Her voice was husky when she answered Jean's cheery "Hello."

"Oh, Jean, the most awful thing has happened to me!" she cried into the telephone. "I won't be in on any of the fun at Crescent Beach this summer. I've got to spend my vacation in Maine with my aunt, at an outlandish place named Bear Paw!"

2. BEAR PAW STATION

THE ENTIRE FAMILY saw April off at the Hartford Railroad Station early on the morning of July fifth. As they clustered on the platform awaiting the arrival of the *Flying Yankee*, the train that would take her as far as Portland, Maine, Mrs. Merriman made a nervous last minute check of April's luggage. The large wardrobe case had gone ahead by express. Even so, April had plenty to manage, what with her topper, small suitcase, shoulder bag, a box of chocolates Daddy had tucked under her arm, a couple of magazines, and a paper-

15

bound "western" novel Perry had bought for her at the magazine stand in the station.

April kept looking in her bag to make sure her ticket was safe. Then, with finicky hands, she would smooth down her tailored beige and brown printed linen dress. Her pumps and belt matched her jade green topper and her hat was a clip of rough brown straw.

"You look very nice," her mother approved.

"Your train goes straight through to Portland," her father told her, as he had told her many times before. "In Portland you change for Bear Paw. Don't be afraid to ask questions," he added as he saw a flash of apprehension in April's eyes. "Anyone working in the station will be glad to direct you."

April's hands felt clammy inside her beige cotton gloves.

"You can eat in the dining car," said her mother. "Or, if you prefer, buy something from the vendors who will come through the train at some of the stations. Don't open your candy until after lunch."

"And don't speak to strangers," grinned Perry.

Then, as the *Flying Yankee* roared into the station, Perry gave April a bearlike hug.

"Chin up, Sis! You're going to have a swell time. Just don't go trying to make up to any moose or bears."

Both April and her mother were close to tears as they kissed good-by.

"My love to Ellen," Mrs. Merriman murmured. "And be sure to send us a note in tomorrow's mail."

Mr. Merriman went into the coach with April, to help her find a seat and to put her suitcase on the rack above the seat. When she was settled, he kissed her and patted her shoulder.

"Okay, Sis?" he asked, his blue eyes anxious now that her travels were actually about to begin.

"Okay, Daddy." April managed a smile.

"You have a delightful summer before you. If you need any more money—or anything—let us know."

He left the train to stand beside Mom and Perry on the platform outside her window. All three wore big smiles. April peered at them yearningly through the thick glass and managed to smile back, but there was a lump in her throat and tears were stinging under her eyelids. Then the train jerked and started up, gradually gathering speed. The last April saw of her family they were still smiling at her and waving. Then the station was left behind and she was on her own!

Daddy always took the family everywhere in his car; this was the first time April had ever been on a train. A middle-aged man sat down beside her. She turned away and stared out of the window, blinking hard to force back her tears. As they crossed the Connecticut River, she saw the early morning mists still floating above the water. The wheels beneath the coach clacked over the track faster and faster. The dazzling July sun, climbing the almost colorless sky, showed the *Flying Yankee* sweeping eastward and northward on the long journey to Maine.

The coach was air-conditioned and comfortable. April soon began to feel a little more relaxed. She looked shyly at her fellow travelers and wondered about them a little. The man next to her was reading a newspaper. April noticed that he had stuck his ticket into the back of the seat ahead. She took her own ticket out of her bag and thrust it into the little slot at the top of the seat. When the conductor came through the train and punched it, she began to feel like a seasoned traveler.

After a while April opened one of the magazines Perry had given her, but most of the time it lay unheeded on her lap while she stared at the landscape outside her window. Towards noon, people began to leave their seats and straggle out to the dining car, but, in spite of a demanding emptiness in her stomach, April was too shy to join the procession. Growing hungrier every second, she waited until they reached the Worcester Station and then bought a chicken sandwich and a carton of milk from a vendor who hawked a tray of food through the train. Later, she opened her box of candy and nibbled chocolates while she turned the pages of the magazine. The rushing panorama of New England countryside outside the train window began to have a wearying effect. April leaned her head against the high back of her seat and closed her eyes. Then she jerked upright in sudden fright.

What if she had fallen asleep and the train had carried her right through Portland to parts unknown!

It was mid-afternoon when the *Flying Yankee* stormed into Portland. After worrying about it all day, April made the change between trains with no trouble at all. Remembering her father's injunction that she ask questions of the station attendants if she felt confused, she discovered with a lift of her heart that people were kindly and friendly, and eager to help her on her way. Safe in her seat on the inland train, she began to take pride in herself as a traveler.

This train was a local which made brief stops at many tiny town and country stations, and a longer pause at the bustling city of Lewiston beside the falls of the Androscoggin River. Peering out of her window, April saw a tall, lanky boy striding along the Lewiston platform; she noted him especially because of his easy, swinging gait. His brown hair was a careless thatch above his bronzed, strong-featured face.

The boy disappeared from view. A few moments later, he came into April's coach and walked along the aisle to the seat opposite hers. Their glances met for an instant; April saw a sudden light of awareness or interest come into his keen gray eyes. He half smiled, then sat down abruptly and stared out the window. Later, glancing his way, she caught the boy looking at her again. She felt her cheeks grow hot. She turned her shoulder to him and did not look toward that side of the train again all the way to Bear Paw.

The train jerked into motion and picked up speed, rattling and swaying, the wheels singing a monotonous song on the rails—clickity-clack, clickity-clack. Towns were further apart now and thick green woods marched along on both sides of the railroad right of way. The sparkle of streams and ponds brightened the landscape. April was suddenly conscious that the sky with its sailing, cottony clouds was a much deeper blue than it had been to the southward. Rolling hills crested with pine reminded her thrillingly that she was in Maine, the Pine Tree State.

The train pushed on and on until April wondered if there could be any end to the state of Maine. She recalled with wonder that when Daddy had showed Bear Paw to her on the map, it had stood about in the center of the state. She was so tired now that her bones felt brittle. There were only a few people left in the coach. Across the aisle the lanky boy lounged comfortably in his seat.

The door of the coach was pushed open and the conductor thrust his head inside.

"Bear Paw Station next stop!"

Her tiredness forgotten, April jumped up as if a spring had suddenly been released. If Bear Paw proved to be one of the mere whistle stops along this track, she must be ready to dash out of the coach to the platform the minute the train slowed down!

Bracing herself against the swaying motion of the coach, she stood on tiptoe to pull her suitcase off the rack above the seat. Hastily she slung the strap of her bag over her shoulder and collected her topper, magazines, and book. As she reached into the corner of the seat for her box of candy, April felt the book slip from under her arm. It pitched into the aisle.

Across the way, the lanky boy unfolded himself and reached out a long arm for the book. He stood up, grinning, as he studied the gaudy cover picture of an Indian and a cowboy shooting at each other from behind rocks.

"I like westerns myself," he confided.

April was embarrassed that this boy should suspect her of choosing such blood-and-thunder reading matter for herself.

"My brother gave it to me to read on the train."

"Shows *his* good taste," the boy said cheerily. He wedged the book under her arm. "Take it easy," he advised, as she staggered off down the aisle with her load. "They wait here ten minutes."

The train jolted to a stop. Thrown off balance by her load, April pitched forward. A strong hand gripped her arm and saved her from a fall. It was the tall boy again. He pulled the suitcase away from her. "Let me."

April pushed through the door of the train and went

21

down the steps to the station platform. The boy followed and set her suitcase down beside her.

She gave him a shy smile. What must he think of her clumsiness!

"Thanks ever so much," she murmured.

"Glad to help." With a friendly wave of his hand, he walked off toward the baggage car.

April spun around, her hazel-green eyes bright with expectancy as they searched the open platform for a glimpse of her aunt.

In the telegram Ellen had sent as soon as she received April's letter accepting her invitation, she had promised to meet this train, but there was not a soul on the platform except the tall boy and two or three men up by the baggage car. April went to peer inside the dingy little waiting room and discovered that it too was deserted. Worriedly she crossed the platform to stare along the village road, which looked as quiet as some lost settlement on the moon.

Directly across from the station was a small pond, with a neat brick building beside it that looked as though it might house an industry of some kind. Further along the road April could see a gas station and a cluster of houses and shops, but, except for a dog trotting along the road, there was not a sign of life. The sun had slid behind the wooded hills to the west and a lingering glow of fire-pink and violet caressed the sky, but down by the station it was beginning to grow dusky.

Panic boiled up inside April. What would she do if Aunt Ellen failed to appear? There did not even seem to be a taxi she could hire to take her to her aunt's cottage—wherever that was!

She repeated the address to herself nervously: Deer Hill Road, care of Charles Oliver.

She walked slowly back to where her things made a lonely heap on the platform and shrugged into her topper. Now that the sun had set, the air had turned suddenly cool, with a nip to it that seemed more like autumn than the fifth of July. A forlorn April huddled down on her suitcase. Even her brown pony tail had a dejected droop.

The station agent was locking up, which meant there would be no more trains that night. April watched the one she had arrived on chug out of the station. The light on the caboose winked smaller and smaller in the distance, and the engine sent its haunting whistle hoo-hooing back through the deepening twilight. April shivered.

For the first time in her life she knew what it meant to be lonely.

"Hello—you still here?" asked a friendly voice.

She glanced up in surprise. It was the lanky boy again. A grin widened his good-humored mouth as he looked at her. She guessed him to be about sixteen—Perry's age.

23

Fervently she wished he wouldn't go away, but her voice was prim. "I'm waiting for someone."

"So am I. Here they come now."

April jumped eagerly to her feet as a car rolled down the road and stopped at the station. Then she sighed with disappointment, for it wasn't Aunt Ellen's car, but instead it was a shabby station wagon. A tall, leggy girl in jeans and a baggy red sweater bounced out. "Hi, Kent!" she called to the boy beside April.

"It's about time you got here, Sis. Hi, Pop!" the boy added as a mild-faced, stoop-shouldered man followed the girl on to the platform.

"Welcome home, Son. How's Grandma?"

"She's fine. Say, Pop, you look tired." There was affectionate solicitude in the look Kent gave his father. "You feeling all right?"

"He's worn out," Sally answered for her father. "He's had a time trying to plow the land for the new orchard. The tractor broke down again."

"It would," Kent said bitterly. "It's practically tied together with string. We'll never get anywhere!" he burst out. "Worn-out land, broken-down tools, and no money to buy new tools or even to get the old junk repaired!"

"Now, Son, don't worry," his father said in an easy-going voice. "Hard work will pull us through."

"Hard work—and with it some modern farm machinery and tons of fertilizer," Kent muttered. "And we don't have enough money to buy chicken feed."

24

The station agent walked over to join their group. "'Evening, Mr. Oliver. Hello, Sally." He looked at April. "Are you expecting someone to come for you, young lady?"

"Yes," April murmured. "My aunt, Miss Ellen Merriman, was supposed to meet me. Something must have happened—"

The tall girl whirled to stare. "Miss Merriman!" she exclaimed. "Why you must be April!" Her words tumbled out gaily. "Oh, this is wonderful. I'm Sally Oliver. Your aunt is living at our place. But she doesn't expect you till tomorrow."

"Oh, no. It was today," April protested.

Sally laughed. There was something so contagious about her high spirits that April found herself laughing too.

"One of you mixed the date," Sally said. "But no matter. You can ride out with us. Won't your aunt be surprised to see you!"

Sally was almost two inches taller than April, although Aunt Ellen had written that they were the same age, fifteen. Something about her reminded April of a frisky fawn she had once seen on television.

Kent Oliver looked as pleased as his sister over the discovery of April's identity. "I should have guessed that you were April Merriman. Sally has been talking of nothing else ever since your aunt told us you were coming to Bear Paw to spend the summer."

25

He picked up April's things and put them in the back of the station wagon, where he also stowed the buckets of paint and boxes of hardware that had been shipped out from Lewiston in the baggage car. Sally and April got into the back seat, and Kent climbed in behind the wheel. His father seemed glad to sit quietly beside him.

"It's good to have you home again, Son," Mr. Oliver said, as Kent started the car.

Sally pointed to the brick building beside the little pond, the one April had noticed earlier. "That is the Bear Paw Woolen Mill," she told April. "Almost everyone in the village works there. Mr. Young, the father of Kent's best friend, owns it."

As the station wagon moved away from the depot, April glanced back at the small mill and its quiet, tree-shaded pond. In her mind she contrasted the peaceful scene with the acres of modern buildings and the hustle and bustle that characterized the vast airplane plants and other industries of Connecticut. She decided that the Bear Paw Woolen Mill seemed a much more pleasant place to work.

The Main Street of Bear Paw was only two blocks long. April noted a small movie theatre, a huge supermarket, and a few other stores. Back among the trees, the white needle of a church spire thrust itself against the evening sky.

"There's the library," Sally said, as they rolled past a

large Victorian house set amid trees and lawns. "The librarian lives upstairs."

The road left the village behind and skirted the shore of a large lake where the first stars were winking back from the tranquil surface of the water.

"Spruce Pond," Kent said over his shoulder. "The good fishing attracts lots of sportsmen. Mik-Chik, our pond, is on the other side of Deer Hill."

He turned the station wagon into another road. They rattled through farm country and then began to climb.

Sally's tongue was going a mile a minute. She explained that Kent had been visiting their grandmother in Lewiston, and buying paint and other supplies needed for the building of a second tourist cabin on their land. Chattering on, she told April that the Oliver family had lived in Bear Paw only since the previous autumn. Before that their home had been in an even smaller, more northerly village, where Mr. Oliver had worked in a sawmill.

"Papa was hurt in an accident. When he got well, the doctor wouldn't let him go back to work in the mill. Mama owned the farm here in Bear Paw, where she had lived as a girl. She'd been renting it, but now we are going to farm it ourselves. The place is awfully run down," Sally confided. "And none of us knows much about farming. That is why Papa and Kent built the cottage where your aunt is staying. We need something to bring in ready cash."

That reminded her of something else. She leaned forward, raising her voice a little.

"Oh, Kent, my pamphlet on worm culture came in yesterday's mail."

Worm culture! April's lips parted a little as she looked in astonishment at the girl beside her. Could she have heard Sally correctly?

"The pamphlet is full of all kinds of valuable tips, both on raising worms and marketing 'em," Sally was saying. "I can go about my business in a scientific fashion now. And who knows? Maybe I'll make us all rich!"

Kent chuckled. "With earthworms? That will be the day!"

Sally laughed too, but her voice was gaily confident. "I have heard all my life about the codfish aristocracy of Boston; well, perhaps someday we Olivers will be known as the earthworm barons of Bear Paw."

She turned back to April, bouncing with enthusiasm.

"I'm raising earthworms to sell to fishermen. Our road connects two lakes. The motorists are always on the lookout for a place to buy fishing worms."

A little shiver of distaste passed over April. But she kept her feelings to herself.

On the other side of the hill the road leveled out. Woods—black, mysterious, and scary to town-bred April—closed in on both sides. A rambling, unlighted, white house was a blur in the darkness as they drove past.

"That's the Alder place—built in seventeen hundred

and something," Sally said, pointing to the house. "No one lives there now."

April's head was whirling. She wondered tiredly if this day's journey would ever end, and if Sally Oliver would ever stop talking!

Lighted windows showed ahead. "That's our house," said Sally.

Kent drove past the farmhouse and the orchard beyond it. Finally he stopped the station wagon where a small space had been cleared in the woods that grew along the road. A car was parked there in the shelter of the trees. "Your aunt's car," said Kent.

April perked up. It was almost like meeting one of the family.

Kent got out. "We have to walk from here. I'll get your things, April."

His father handed him a flashlight.

April stared into the shadowy woods. Was it possible that Aunt Ellen was living somewhere in that lonely wilderness of trees? Except for the windows of the Oliver house, they had not seen a light since they had come over the hill.

"Ready, April?" said Kent.

April stepped out of the car and murmured thanks and good night to Sally and Mr. Oliver. Then she stumbled after Kent, who kept shining the light back so she could see the narrow path they were following through the woods. Enormous pines towered above them, their faraway tips whispering against the star-splintered sky. April thought wildly of moose and bears. She crowded so close to Kent's heels that she almost walked over him. After a while they climbed a knoll and saw a light sparkling ahead. April made out the dark outline of a cottage. A whiff of wood smoke mingled with the cool night scent of the forest.

Kent knocked at the cottage door. "Miss Merriman!"

The door opened. A tall young woman in a quilted nylon duster was framed in the oblong of light. "Why Kent—come in," she said hospitably, pushing open the screen door.

He stepped back. "Here's April. Pa and Sally picked both of us up at the station."

"Hello, Aunt Ellen," April said faintly.

"April!" Ellen Merriman's lovely face registered bewilderment. "But I thought you wouldn't arrive until tomorrow! Oh, come in, dear. Welcome to Deer Hill."

She pulled April into the cottage and kissed her warmly.

Kent carried April's suitcase and topper inside.

"I am so glad to be here at last!" April exclaimed, hugging her aunt in grateful appreciation of having finally come to the end of her journey. "For a while I thought I wouldn't make it," she added with a laugh.

"Do forgive me for not meeting you at the train," Ellen said contritely. "How could I have gotten so mixed up on the date of your arrival? I lost your letter, but for some reason the sixth was the day fixed in my mind. I hate to think of how your mother will feel about this. It's a lucky thing that Kent happened to be getting back tonight."

She turned to Kent, to thank him, but he had quietly left the cottage and was walking back down the trail.

3. THE FRIENDLY OLIVERS

THERE WAS A PIQUANT SCENT to the nippy air the following morning that made April smile even while she was only half awake. She sniffed eagerly. Mmm—pine and balsam! Crescent Beach had never smelled like *this*.

She turned over in bed and stretched like a cat. Then suddenly she was wide awake and she sat up in bed and looked around the strange room.

It was a tiny room with walls of clean new pine. The plain furniture was maple: a single bed, a chair, and a chest of drawers with a mirror hanging over it. There was a hand-braided rug on the floor by the bed. The sliding window took up almost all of one wall; it was curtained with pull drapes of red cotton with a blithe provincial print. The drapes were well apart so that April could look out into the woods. All the tall trees in the world seemed to be out there!

April sat clasping her knees, staring out into the green woods and thinking about how very far she was from home and all that was dear and familiar. A wave of such poignant homesickness swept over her that she felt faint and ill. She put her head down on her knees and squeezed her eyes tight shut. She did not want to look at the trees, or get out of bed, or do anything but just go home.

"Breakfast in ten minutes!" Ellen called cheerily from outside the bedroom door.

April lifted her head. She tried to make her voice as carefree as her aunt's.

"Coming, Aunt Ellen."

She hopped out of bed, grabbed her corduroy robe, and dashed into the cubbyhole of a bathroom which connected the two bedrooms. In the shower she let out a howl as a deluge of icy water cascaded over her. Tingling and wide awake, she ran back to her room and hustled into her clothes: green Bermuda skirt, knitted blouse striped in coral and two shades of green, and pigskin sport shoes. With her robe over her shoulders, she stood before the little mirror and brushed a coppery sheen into her brown hair. Mom had given her a home permanent before she had left on this trip; the wave had turned out well, April thought with pleasure. She used her fingers to curl up the bang over her broad, smooth forehead, and tied her pony tail with a coral ribbon.

The good odors of breakfast cooking sharpened April's appetite as she opened the door into the main room of the cottage.

The big room had wide, sliding windows in two walls. The windows seemed to bring the green woods inside. There was a floor-length window in the third wall, opening on the screened porch. The room was separated into living room and kitchen areas by the huge fieldstone chimney that went up through the center of the low roof. There was a fireplace in the living room side of the chimney; around the chimney in the kitchen end, a small wood-burning range was sending out a welcome glow. As in the bedroom, everything here was bright and new. The pine boards in wall and floor gave out a clean, aromatic scent.

Sausages were browning in a frying pan. At the cupboard counter Ellen was mixing pancakes. The early sun shone through the windows to tangle in the pale gold of her curly ash-blonde hair. She looked up from her work to smile at April.

"Good morning, dear. It seems so good to have you here with me."

April felt a guilty pang because of her secret unwillingness to be here. She went over to kiss her aunt.

"You were sweet to ask me," she said sincerely. She looked toward the range. "Mmm. Those sausages smell good. And the fire feels good! Is it always this cold, mornings in Maine?"

"It will warm up beautifully by midday." Ellen's larkspur blue eyes twinkled at her. "I heard you yell in the shower. I should have warned you that we have spring water here—icy cold. When you want a hot bath there's a little tub you fill and heat on the stove." She tested the griddle and poured out dough for four cakes. "Will you please get the butter and syrup from the refrigerator, April?"

April found the things and carried them to the table by the window. Ellen had already set the table with brown pottery dishes.

Seeing the small electric refrigerator tucked into a corner of the kitchen had surprised April.

"I wondered how you would manage to keep butter and milk fresh in this isolated spot," she told Ellen.

Ellen chuckled. "I wondered about that myself when I first arrived here, and was I glad to see that refrigerator! It seems electricity goes everywhere these days, with the accompanying blessings of running water and refrigeration."

April was peering out of the window in the hope of seeing a glimmer of water, but there were only the tall pines and hemlocks sifting their sun-laced shade over the fern-grown clearing.

"How far is it to the lake, Aunt Ellen?"

"About a mile." Ellen whisked the delicately browned cakes from the griddle to a plate. "You reach it by an old tote road that branches off Deer Hill Road right across from our mailbox. It's a lovely walk through deep woods all the way."

She poured out more pancake batter, and then carried the cakes that were already baked to the table and took her place opposite April.

"I haven't been in swimming yet. I'm still waiting for the water to warm up." Ellen looked at April seriously.

"Remember, I do not want you going swimming by yourself—ever."

April nodded. She had no intention of going anywhere in the woods by herself.

"Sally will go with you sometimes," Ellen continued, as April jumped up to turn the second batch of hot cakes and bring them to the table. "Kent tells me she is a very good swimmer."

After helping with the breakfast dishes and tidying her room, April wrote a letter home announcing her safe arrival at Bear Paw, but not mentioning that Ellen had failed to meet her train. Then she wrote a note to Jean, who was now at Crescent Beach. She sighed as she stamped the envelopes. By now all the families except the Merrimans would be established in their cottages at the beach, and summer activities would be in full swing. And here she was in the middle of the big woods, missing all the fun and excitement! She wasn't even close enough to the lake to be able to go swimming often. The weeks of summer stretched before her, dull and uneventful.

Ellen told her she could mail the letters in the box on Deer Hill Road at the beginning of their path.

"Then perhaps you'd like to walk over to the farmhouse and get some butter and fresh vegetables. Sally usually brings them, but I happen to know that today she and her mother are busy canning."

April put on her sweater and took the basket Ellen offered her. At the door she paused to peer out worriedly through the screen that separated her from the green mystery of the woods.

"What if I meet a moose?" she said in a small voice.

Ellen came to stand beside her. "Kent told me that moose and bears are rarely seen on this side of the pond —they prefer the wild country over on the other side, where there are no houses at all, and but few trails. Kent seems to be very woods-wise," she added. "He assured me that wild animals are no more anxious to meet us than we are to meet them. With their keen hearing and sense of smell, they are able to discover the presence of humans a long way off in the woods and they keep out of our way."

April drew a deep breath and stepped out into the sparkling morning.

As she started down the trail she glanced about nervously, half expecting to see a moose or wildcat lurking behind every tree. A little brown bunny, hopping into view around a juniper bush, startled her almost out of her wits. Then she let out a trill of delighted laughter as the rabbit paused to scratch vigorously behind one floppy ear with a hind foot. With an indignant twinkle of its fluffy tail, the rabbit bounced off into the woods. As April stood gazing after it, a pert chipmunk ran over her foot and dove frantically into a hole beneath a mossy log.

Why—these creatures were afraid of *her!*

"I won't hurt you," April murmured, stooping to peer into the chipmunk hole.

A shade less nervous now, she strode on her way, breathing deep of the pine-laden air. The path, which had seemed so rugged and steep in the dark the night before, was only a gentle slope in the morning light. She was surprised at what a short distance it was to where her aunt's car was parked beside Deer Hill Road.

The words *Deer Hill Camp* were lettered on the metal mailbox set on a post at the end of the path. Across the road were dense green woods, but beyond a fringe of trees on the camp side was an apple orchard, with a rambling red farmhouse showing further up the road.

April put her letters in the box and, as Aunt Ellen had told her to do, she raised the little red flag to signal the mailman when he came on his rounds. Then, swinging her basket, she walked up the road toward the farm-house.

Now that she was out of the woods she felt quite safe and confident; somehow she could not picture a deep-woods creature like a moose ambling along this sunny country road.

As she was passing the orchard, a flash of brilliant blue wings caught her attention. At first she thought it was a bluejay, familiar even to her urban eyes, but this bird looked even bluer than a jay, if that were possible. She stood at the edge of the orchard and peered in among the trees. After a few moments she again glimpsed the glitter of blue wings. The bird lighted on a branch close enough to give her a clear view of it. She saw that it had a rusty red breast.

A bluebird! She had seen plenty of them in pictures, but to see a live one on her first morning in Maine was surely a good omen. At any rate it gave her a sense of well-being.

As she started along the road again, the bluebird's liquid song floated after her.

Chur-ri. Chur-ri.

"Cheery! Cheery!" April sang back.

She was humming under her breath as she walked into the yard of the farmhouse, but the next minute she stopped short in terror at the sight of a big black dog lying in the sun on the Olivers' kitchen doorstone. The dog rose bristling from his place and started toward her, stiff-legged and growling.

"Go away! Go away!" April shrilled, holding the basket before her as a shield.

The dog began to bark at her. She screamed. Terror froze her to the spot.

The kitchen door banged. Sally came pelting down the path, a big gingham apron tied over her jeans.

"Pete! Stop that!"

The dog ceased his noise, but he continued to keep an alert watch on April. He was a handsome fellow, his heavy black coat feathered with russet down his sturdy legs, like the fringe on an Indian's leggings.

"I'm sorry he frightened you, April. Pete is very conscientious about guarding the farm." Sally smoothed the dog's silky ears. "April is a friend, Pete."

Pete began to wag his tail.

"Shake hands to show you are friends," Sally suggested.

The setter raised a big black paw and looked expectant.

April backed away. "Oh, no—I couldn't."

She had never touched a dog or cat in her life.

"Please do," Sally insisted. "Then you won't ever have to be afraid of him again."

She stood with one hand on Pete's head, her eyes as soft and brown as those of the Gordon setter.

April didn't want Sally to despise her for a coward.

Swallowing hard, she walked over to Pete and took his paw timidly. "N—nice dog," she faltered.

She dropped the paw and stepped back quickly, surprised that he hadn't nipped her fingers. More confident now, she dared a light pat on the dog's head. "Nice dog," she murmured.

And this time she meant it.

Sally gave her a warm smile. "Now come and meet Mama. Then you'll know the whole family except Tinkerbell."

Pete whined softly.

"Who is Tinkerbell?" April asked as they walked up the path.

"She's our cat. She has gone off somewhere to have her kittens—been away four days. Pete misses her dreadfully." Sally pushed the screen door open. "We're making jelly."

Mrs. Oliver, a handsome, motherly woman, was at the huge black range skimming a kettle of boiling jelly. She asked April to be seated in the Boston rocker by the open window, away from the heat of the wood-burning range. Sally fetched from the pantry some tender young carrots, a head of crisp new lettuce, a pound of butter, and a loaf of fresh-baked bread and packed them in April's basket.

The kitchen was hot and steamy from the brisk wood fire and the boiling jelly. April could not help but notice that the furniture was worn and shabby and the linoleum rug was scuffed and faded. There were no curtains at the windows and the shades were stained and yellow with age. Suddenly she realized with amazement that there was an iron hand pump at one end of the black sink. Evidently the Olivers could not afford to have running water in their house, although they had installed it in the cottage they rented out! Mentally April contrasted this room with her mother's beautiful all-electric kitchen at home.

But here, as at home, everything was as clean and scrubbed as could be.

Outside, Pete gave a short, excited bark.

"Meow!" cried a demanding cat voice. Claws raked across the screen door.

"It's Tinkerbell!" cried Sally.

She ran to open the door. In walked a big, gray-brown cat, bushy tail held high and proud. Pete crowded in after her.

Sally hastened to set down a saucer of cream and a generous portion of cat food. The cat rubbed fondly against her and then went at the food in a businesslike way. Pete settled down nearby, his head on his paws. Once, when his black nose advanced too close to her plate, the cat growled and gave him a warning pat with her paw. Pete drew back, his pink tongue curling out in a grin, as if he thought this very funny. April watched them with mounting interest. It was surprising to her to see such friendship between a cat and dog.

42

"Tinker is a coon cat, 'shags' some people call them," said Sally. "They are found only in Maine. There's a legend that a Maine sea captain once brought home an Angora cat, and that she wandered into the woods and mated with a raccoon. Her kittens were the first coon cats."

"Some folks say that story is pure nonsense," put in Mrs. Oliver, testing the jelly.

"You keep Tinker in during the hunting season because you're afraid someone will shoot her for a raccoon," Sally reminded her.

"The markings are very similar. Well, it could be there is truth in the old tale," her mother conceded.

The girls went outside and Sally led the way around behind the woodshed.

"I want to show you my worm flats."

A number of wooden butter tubs, filled with rich soil, were ranged beneath the sloping jut of the roof.

"Here is where I keep my little pets, with cans handy to put 'em in whenever a customer calls." Sally waved her hand toward a pile of empty tin cans.

"Worms! Ugh!" April's face mirrored her loathing.

Sally laughed. "You see," she said, as they started back to the front yard, "'way out here I can't baby-sit or do anything like that to earn money. I had to think of something. Then I read an article in a magazine about two women carrying on a brisk business raising and selling earthworms. There is a chain of lakes and ponds in this region, linking Kennebec country with Androscoggin country; Indians used it in the old days, going from one river to the other, and today it is a fisherman's paradise. Loads of fishermen pass by here, and fishermen are always looking for fresh bait. Worms bring three cents apiece."

"Three cents for a common old earthworm!"

"A fishing worm," Sally corrected. "A good lively one that bass and trout will go for. It makes all the difference in the world."

The girls walked back to retrieve April's basket from where she had left it in the cool shade of the grapevine near the kitchen door. Pete was sitting forlornly on the doorstone.

"Tinkerbell slipped away again," Mrs. Oliver called through the screen.

"Oh, dear!" Sally sighed worriedly. "She must have her babies tucked away in a cave or hollow tree. I'm afraid a fox or owl will find them. But it is useless to try to trail Tinker, she is a fox herself when she wants to steal away."

Sally strolled with April as far as the road. Kent was nailing a sign to a maple tree near the entrance to the driveway. A huge red earthworm was painted across the top of the board. Under it black letters shouted:

Buy Fishing Worms Here! 3¢ Each.

"There you are, Sis," Kent said, stepping back to study the sign. "Pretty effective, eh? My fee is some sample worms for fishing."

He smiled at April from his rangy height. April decided that Kent was much better looking than she had thought him the night before; there was a good-humored quirk to his generous mouth, and his gray eyes seemed to reflect all the light of the summer morning. But she still had to admit that his rough-hewn features could never be called handsome.

This morning he wore blue jeans, faded and patched, and a blue chambray shirt thin with age. He looked as though he had already put in a strenuous day's work on the farm.

"Want to walk down to the pond this afternoon, April?" Kent asked. "Sis can come too if she promises not to talk all the time."

Sally gave April a sparkling glance. "There is something at the pond I've been dying to show you ever since I heard you were coming to Maine for the summer."

Sally refused to even hint at what the "something" might be. April wondered about it all the while she and Ellen were eating lunch. She thought about the Olivers too. Missing Jean as she did, how lucky she was to find such a friendly girl as Sally Oliver living right next door in this out-of-the-way place. Sally was so alive that every minute spent with her seemed like a jolly adventure. Why she even managed to make earthworms seem interesting!

The thought of Sally's hobby made April wrinkle her nose.

"What is it?" asked Ellen, across the table. "Don't you like fruit salad?"

"The salad is scrumptious," April hastened to assure her. "I was thinking about earthworms."

Ellen laughed. "What a subject for the luncheon table."

"Sally raises them to make money," April explained. She looked gravely at her aunt. "The Olivers seem to be awfully poor."

Ellen gave a sympathetic little nod. "They have had a lot of bad luck. And now they are finding it a struggle to make a fresh start on this run-down farm of theirs. But they are all hard workers—they'll come through all right. It is a pity Mr. Oliver's health is so poor," she added. "Kent carries a heavy load for a boy his age."

"I know," said April. "You can't be with Kent two minutes without realizing how much he worries about his father, and the farm too."

She thought about the difference between Perry's and her own outlook on life from that of the young Olivers. She and Perry never had a thought other than that Daddy was perfectly capable of taking care of the family. Of course they had plans for the future: she wanted to be a librarian, like Aunt Ellen; and after college Perry would probably go into his father's law firm. But neither of

46

them had ever had a real worry. She thought about the generous allowance Daddy handed her every week, and then, with a new and humble sense of her own inadequacy, of how Sally Oliver earned her own money. Anxiously she wondered whether, if trouble should come to their family, she and Perry would be able to take hold and help, as Sally and Kent were doing. After a moment she decided that Perry, for all his breezy air, would be a rock in time of need.

But why such gloomy notions? No hard times threatened; if they came she would do her part as best she could—like Sally and Kent.

"Are you planning anything for this afternoon, Aunt Ellen?" April asked, as they were doing the luncheon dishes. "Kent and Sally asked me to walk down to the pond with them."

"Go by all means," Ellen replied cheerfully. "I feel indolent today; I'll just laze under the pines and read. Tomorrow we'll take the car and go exploring, see some of the other lakes, and find some nice inn where we can have lunch."

"That will be fun," April agreed with enthusiasm.

4. MIK-CHIK POND

SALLY ARRIVED SOON after lunch, bringing a jar of
fresh strawberry jelly for Ellen.

"Kent is waiting for us on the road," she told April, as
they started down the path. "His friend, Chuck Young,
is coming out from Bear Paw to go fishing with us.
You'll like Chuck."

Sally wore her jeans, scuffed brown loafers, and
a clean, cotton plaid shirt. Her red-brown hair was short
except where it crisped into waves about her forehead.
Her complexion was like smooth cream with a rich wash
of rose on her high cheekbones. April thought Sally was

the prettiest girl she had ever seen. But she wondered if the farm girl didn't have anything to wear but those shabby jeans.

Kent was sprawled on the roadside bank near the mailbox, his arm around Pete's neck. There was an old steel fishing rod beside him, a tin can full of worms, and a chunk of salt pork on top of the can. He sat up and gave April a companionable smile. Pete greeted her by thrusting his moist black nose into her hand.

A warm tide of pleasure swept over April. Never before had an animal made up to her. Still a little timid, she gently stroked Pete's silky black head.

Sally was looking up the road. "Here comes a car. Perhaps it's Chuck."

Kent got to his feet. "George Crawly is giving Chuck a lift out here. They want to talk to me about something."

"George Crawly!" Sally made a face. "What does *he* want?"

"His dad has opened a gas station in Bear Paw. Could be they're going to offer Chuck and me jobs for the summer." Kent's usually pleasant face set in grim lines. "We could use some ready cash in our family. We'll never make a go of farming until we can get some modern machinery, and the place is so heavily mortgaged already that we can't even raise a loan on it. If I could get a job—"

"You can't leave Papa, sick as he is, to do all the work at home by himself," Sally reminded him.

Kent nodded unhappily.

"And Chuck doesn't need a job with that George Crawly," Sally went on scornfully. "He can go to work any time in his father's mill."

"That would be too tame for Chuck," Kent said with a laugh.

The shabby car rattled up to them and stopped. "Hi, gang!" hailed a jolly voice. A stocky youth with his hair in a crew cut jumped out of the seat beside the driver. He was carrying a fishing rod in a case and a metal tackle box.

Sally gave him a welcoming smile. "Hello, Chuck."

"How's my girl?" He flung an arm around her.

She stepped away, but it was easy to see that she was not displeased. She turned to April. "This is Charles Young. And this is April Merriman, Chuck. She's staying at Deer Hill Cottage."

Chuck had a broad, friendly smile. "Glad to know you, April." He stooped to rumble Pete's silky ears. "How are you, Pete, old feller?"

But Pete was watching the car. His lips were drawn back from his gleaming teeth in a thin snarl.

"Pete hates George Crawly," Sally whispered to April. "George kicked Tinker once, when he was at our place. It took Kent and me together to hold Pete so George could get away in one piece. You notice George doesn't dare get out of the car with Pete here."

April glanced briefly at the narrow-faced young man behind the wheel of the car. He had a mean look, she decided, but perhaps that was because his eyes were set so close on either side of his sharp nose.

"Hey, Chuck," George called. "Come here and tell Kent how you feel about my proposition."

Chuck joined Kent by the car door and the three talked earnestly in low tones.

"I'll see you in a few days, Kent," George said finally, loud enough for the girls to hear. "You make up your mind by then."

Kent wore a troubled frown. "I don't like it."

"You think it over," George insisted.

"About time we had a little excitement around here," Chuck added.

George turned the car around and drove back up the road.

"I thought we were going fishing," Sally called tartly to Kent and Chuck, who still had their heads together over whatever it was they had been discussing with George Crawly.

Sally and April started slowly down the shady tote road that penetrated the thick woods across from the mail box. After a moment, Kent and Chuck followed, still whispering together.

"What's the big secret?" Sally demanded over her shoulder. "What did George want?"

"If we told you, you'd know," Kent teased.

A long stride took him beside April. He tilted his fishing rod over his shoulder and began to whistle. Behind them Chuck and Sally were clowning and laughing. Pete coursed ahead, nosing out bird scents.

Dim greenish light sifted through the high branches of the pines. Underfoot, tiny firs and hemlocks were pushing up through thick, emerald-green moss and mats of partridgeberry vines where scarlet berries shone like jewels among the delicate leaves. Down ahead was the blue sparkle of water.

April gazed about with a feeling of enchantment. "Do you own these woods?" she asked Kent.

He shook his head. "All this land, back to Deer Hill Road, and three miles of lake front, belongs to the Alder family, the folks who own that old house up the road."

"There is only one of them left now," Chuck put in. "Jim Alder. He's a cousin of mine. He went away from Bear Paw years ago, but he sends Dad a check every year to pay the taxes on his property. One check came from Alaska. The last one was from some place in Central America. He writes travel books—good ones."

"Oh!" April cried, thrilled. "Is he the Jim Alder who wrote *Alaskan Snows* and *The Treasure of Yucatan?*"

"Yep. That's Cousin Jim."

April looked at Chuck with new respect. To think that

she was actually out walking with a cousin of Jim Alder's!

Pete, who was ranging in front of them, began to bark wildly. Up from a bed of fern, in a thicket of white birches beside the pond, sprang a big buck with antlers still in velvet. The young people had a moment's sharp view of him silhouetted against the brightness of the blue pond, then he cleared the bank in a superb leap and splashed into the water. Swimming strongly, he headed for the opposite shore.

"Will he make it?" April cried, one hand at her throat.

"Deer are good swimmers," Sally assured her.

But they all watched anxiously until the deer heaved himself out of the water on the far shore. There was a streak of red-brown across the narrow beach and then the forest closed behind him in his flight. April found herself trembling. Chill after chill raced down her spine. Strangely, because she had never been happier, her eyes filled with tears.

"Well!" Sally exclaimed. "It almost seems as though that deer put on a show especially for April."

"These woods are full of deer," Chuck said matter-of-factly.

Kent walked down to where an ancient rowboat was turned upside-down under some bushes on the bank. "We can't use this today," he said, inspecting it. "Seams need caulking."

"We'll fish from the wharf," Chuck said.

Kent nodded and stood up. "I'll repair the old tub soon, so you and Sally can go rowing," he told April.

The little cove, where the tote road ended, was spangled with water lilies. Purple pickerel weed and gleaming white flowers of arrowhead fringed the shallows. The boys walked to the end of a sagging wharf, built out over huge boulders to deep water. Chuck took his handsome casting rod out of its case and fitted it together. Kent pulled a paper of hooks and a cheap reel from the pocket of his jeans. He strung up swiftly and had his line in the water while Chuck was still pawing through the stuff in his tackle box, debating which expensive lure to use.

"We'll see you later," Sally told the boys.

Her brown eyes were dancing as she looked at April. "And now for my surprise!" She was glowing with eagerness.

Sally leading, they walked single file along a faint trail that followed the shore of the pond.

"I want to show you a place I found last winter when I was down here gathering Christmas greens," Sally said over her shoulder.

Tall pines and dark spruce, tangy scented balsam and gleaming white birch trees crowded close to the trail. Blue flashes of pond water showed through the thickly clustered branches. Presently they came out into a small clearing on the lake shore. April stopped short, her lips parted, her eyes wide.

"Oh!" she cried in delight.

Tucked under the trees was a tiny cabin. It's weathered log walls, squatty stone chimney, and moss-covered roof made it look as though it had grown there, like a forest toadstool.

"Chuck told me that Jim Alder built this cabin when he was a boy, with the help of an old guide of his father's," Sally said, as they crossed the clearing. "He used to live down here by himself in the summer for weeks at a time, when he was our age. And he wrote his first book in this cabin."

This bit of information gave the cabin the ultimate touch of romance as far as April was concerned. She brushed her fingers along the logs of the walls as though she couldn't believe that they were real.

A wooden peg, thrust through an iron hasp, fastened the door. Sally pulled it out and pushed the door open on its rusty hinges.

"I didn't open the door when I was here alone," she confessed.

Standing on the threshold, the girls peeked into the single small room. Heavy wooden blinds over the glassless windows made the light dim inside. They could see faintly that two bunks were built against opposite walls. There were benches made of puncheons mounted on rough-hewn logs, an unpainted table, and some empty shelves. The fieldstone fireplace took up most of the wall opposite the door.

The bunks and shelves held a litter of brown leaves and dried grasses, and there were little piles of acorns, pinecones, and beechnuts. Shells were strewn about everywhere. The fireplace was choked with leaves and the charred remains of long-dead fires. The uneven board floor was messy and littered like the bunks.

After a moment Sally ventured into the room. April tagged behind her, wrinkling her nose against the cold, stale, musty smell of the room.

"It smells of mice in here," said Sally.

April beat a swift retreat to the door.

"Woodmice," Sally added. "Cute little fellows." She pointed to the nest of grass in the corner of one of the bunks. "They must live in here during the winter—but they will all have moved back outdoors by this time. Squirrels have been here too."

She kicked at the shells on the floor.

"It sure does smell terrible in here!" April said.

She stood near the door, ready to flee if a mouse so much as showed a whisker.

"It needs airing," said Sally. "And it would be easy to clean."

Standing with hands on her slim hips, she gave April a bright glance from her merry brown eyes.

"Think of how cozy this cabin could be if we fixed it up! There's some old screening in our tool shed that could be nailed over the windows."

Now what in the world is she getting at? April wondered.

"Ever since I found this place, I've been just crazy to camp down here in the woods, even if it's only for a week," Sally confided. "Mama would not let me come alone, and I don't think I'd want to anyhow. But now that you're here—"

"Me!" April stared at her.

"Oh, April, it would be such fun!"

"But—but—" April quailed to think of what it would be like down here after dark. Two girls in a howling wilderness with wildcats and moose for neighbors.

"We could cook our meals in the fireplace," Sally planned eagerly. "Mornings and evenings we'd be right here to watch the deer when they come to the pond."

"It might be fun." In spite of her doubts April was catching some of Sally's ardor.

Sally stamped her foot on one of the wide floor boards. "The floor is still sound. And the roof is tight— there's no sign of any leakage. There's nothing wrong with this cabin that airing and a good scrubbing won't remedy."

She followed April outside and turned to fasten the cabin door. Then she linked her arm in April's as they walked across the clearing.

"Well? How about it?" she asked hopefully.

I've been a sissy and a city slicker all my life, April thought, but she felt a stirring of enthusiasm for Sally's scheme. Perry is right, it's high time I broke out of my glass case and had some adventures of my own!

Aloud, she said, "I'd love to come down here and

camp with you, Sally. I'll ask Aunt Ellen tonight if it will be all right with her."

Sally did a jig in the middle of the trail, stubbed her toe on a root, and stumbled forward to fall flat on her face.

"Are you hurt?" April cried anxiously, bending over her.

"No—only clumsy," Sally groaned, her face pressed against the soft mat of needles and tiny ferns. She sat up, laughing and rubbing her nose. "Lucky I picked a soft spot!" She got lightly to her feet. "I'm all right—but even a broken nose couldn't dampen my spirits just now."

She looked as if she were going to do another dance, but April grabbed her arm and gave her a little push along the trail.

"Calm down, Sally," she begged. "You don't want to break your nose or something before we get a chance to camp in Jim Alder's cabin!"

When the girls came in sight of the lily cove, they saw Chuck on the narrow strip of beach cleaning the string of white perch and crappies he and Kent had caught. Kent was still casting from the end of the wharf.

"Let's not tell them about our plans for the cabin until everything is settled," Sally whispered.

April nodded.

"Time to start for home," Sally called to Kent. "Evening chores!"

Kent started to reel in his line. Standing on the bank of the pond near the wharf, April could see the bit of salt pork on the hook flash through the water. And suddenly she was aware of something else that had appeared out there in the rippling green shadow cast by the trees. A sinister looking head, big as her fist!

Chuck, who was washing the fish, spotted the evil, reptilian head at the same instant. He jumped to his feet.

"Holy smoke! Look at the size of that turtle!"

The huge head of the snapping turtle disappeared, but the watchers could see a furious boiling of the water as he lunged for the strip of salt pork and clamped his jaws upon it. The hook, a large one meant for fighting pickerel, bit into his horny mouth, sending him plunging to the bottom of the pond. Kent let out a yell as the turtle's weight and power bent the flexible steel rod almost double. Skillfully he played out the line; then he checked the humming reel and slowly began to draw the immense snapper back to the surface. The monster fought every inch of the way, but the pressure on its mouth continued to pull it relentlessly toward the wharf.

Chuck was hopping up and down in his excitement. "Biggest turtle I ever saw!" he yelped. "Don't lose him, Kent!"

Breathing deeply, Kent backed along the wharf to the bank, keeping his rod tip high and still winding in line. Responding unwillingly to the firm pull of the line, the big turtle crawled out of the water on its thick legs, its heavy tail dragging, its savage head high because of the pressure of the hook.

April retreated a few steps. The snapping turtle, dirty gray in color, its muddy shell covered with algae, was an ugly, fearsome object, yet her heart tightened with pity.

"Let it go!" she begged. "That hook must hurt it awfully."

Kent threw her a quick glance. "It feels the pull, but no hurt," he explained. "Its mouth is too hard to feel any pain from the hook. Turn him over, Chuck!"

Chuck ran for a stout branch. With a quick thrust under the turtle's broad plastron, he flipped the creature over on its back. The turtle lay helpless, its four stout legs in the air. A deep, mournful sounding sigh escaped from it. The sigh found an echo in April's heart.

Kent kept the line taut so the turtle could not pull its head inside the shell. Chuck whipped out his handkerchief, pulled a red bandanna from Kent's hip pocket, and knotted the two together. This rope he tied around the turtle's tail; then he stood up and held the reptile warily at arm's length while Kent took out his knife and cut the fishing line. The turtle was hissing and snapping, and twisting its fearsome head on its long neck. The boys dared not venture close enough to extract the hook from its sharp jaws.

"He could take off a couple of fingers as easily as a meat slicer," Kent told April.

She could not bear to look at the captive turtle.

"What are you going to do with him?"

"Sell him to the inn at Bear Paw. Turtle soup is a delicacy, you know. They'll keep him alive in a barrel of water until they're ready to cook him."

"Ugh." April could not imagine anyone relishing soup made from such a repulsive creature.

"I wouldn't turn him loose in the pond again even if there were no market for turtles," Kent went on, as he and April followed Sally and Chuck and the big turtle up the tote road. Kent was carrying the fishing rods and Chuck's tackle box. Sally had one string of fish and April was gingerly carrying the other. "Snappers eat ducklings and even grown birds, as well as bass and other fish. The wild ducks and loons of Mik-Chik Pond will thank me for ridding them of this terror."

April shuddered as she looked at the savage creature Chuck was holding so cautiously at arm's length. Vicious though he was, she knew she could never be the one to take the snapping turtle's life.

"Don't forget to ask your aunt about you know what," Sally reminded April, when they parted company near the cottage on Deer Hill Road.

Kent looked from one girl to the other. "What's this?" he demanded. "A secret?"

April laughed and nodded. "A deep, dark secret between Sally and me and the chipmunks."

5. THE OLD ALDER PLACE

AT THE SUPPER TABLE that night April eagerly described the old cabin to her aunt.

"Sally has wonderful plans for a week of camping down there—just the two of us," she added in a glow of enthusiasm. "Do you think I might go, Aunt Ellen? Would you mind awfully if I left you by yourself for just a week?"

Ellen looked amazed, then doubtful. "It isn't that I would mind, dear," she said after a moment. "I want you to enjoy yourself, but it is rather startling to think of you and Sally going off into the woods by yourselves.

Wouldn't it be almost as much fun if you stayed at the cabin daytimes and came home at night?"

"Oh, no. That wouldn't be the same at all. We want to live like pioneers, and who ever heard of Daniel Boone running home to his aunt at sunset?"

"But just the two of you at night," Ellen demurred. "If something should happen—"

"Sally says it is perfectly safe."

April had become so zealous for the camping adventure that she had almost forgotten her fear of the woods. Something stronger than fear had flowered inside her during this eventful first day in Maine: a growing awareness of the wonders of the forest world, and an urgent desire to learn more about its thrilling secrets.

"Sally says the only thing to be afraid of is fire," she continued, "and we'll be plenty careful of that, you bet."

During the train ride to Bear Paw, April had seen the dismal black ruins left by a vast forest fire that had swept across the land. She knew she would never be able to forget the pitiful charcoal desolation of stumps and spars that was all that remained of once magnificent trees.

"There is a fireplace in the cabin and we'll cook there, never in the woods." Her dark-lashed hazel eyes looked pleadingly at her aunt.

Whenever Ellen smiled, a single enchanting dimple showed at one corner of her pretty mouth. She reached across the table and patted April's hand.

"I don't want to spoil your fun, but, really, I think I should talk this over with Mrs. Oliver before I give my consent. About this cabin," she added, "would the owner be willing for you to stay there?"

"We can't ask him because he isn't here. You know who owns that cabin, Aunt Ellen? And the old white house up the road? Jim Alder. The author of *The Treasure of Yucatan*."

Ellen's eyes brightened with interest. "That book was one of last year's best sellers. I enjoyed it enormously —Jim Alder is one of my favorite writers. So he lived here in Bear Paw!"

"As a matter of fact he's Chuck Young's cousin. Chuck is a friend of Kent's—I met him this afternoon," April informed her. "Chuck's father is looking after the Alder property. Sally is going to ask him for permission to camp in the cabin—that is, if you and Mrs. Oliver agree to let us go."

She gave her aunt another appealing look. If the camping trip failed to come off, she knew she'd really be terribly disappointed.

The next day when Ellen and April drove to the village for groceries, Ellen slowed the car as they approached the Alder place. She and April stared at the rambling, tightly shuttered old farmhouse with new interest now that they knew a favorite author had spent his boyhood there. Dark spruces and stately maples dappled the white walls with lacy shadows. Sunlight glittered on the graceful fanlight over the wide front door.

"It's a handsome old house," said Ellen. "If it were mine, I don't think I'd care to spend my life roaming about in distant places."

April's attention was caught by something moving in the tall grass in the yard. "Please stop!" she cried to Ellen.

Ellen put on the brake. "What's the matter?" Then she too saw the bushy-tailed animal. "It's a raccoon."

"No. It's Tinkerbell, Sally's coon cat. She must have her kittens hidden somewhere about this place. Sally is awfully worried about those kittens. Maybe we can find them for her."

April got out of the car and ran along the driveway. Tinkerbell had disappeared behind a clump of lilacs that grew at the corner of the one-story ell at the rear of the house, but when April reached the lilacs there was no sign of the cat. April stared in dismay at the closed house, and at the various outbuildings and the big red barn at the end of the driveway. The kittens could be almost anywhere; just where to look first was the problem.

Ellen joined her as she was peering into the open woodshed at the end of the ell porch. "A deserted barn would seem like a good place to hide kittens. Cats have a way of getting in where they want to go."

The big central doors of the barn were padlocked, but around at the side they found a small door that opened readily at their touch. When they stood inside the barn, April realized that finding kittens in there would be an almost impossible task. Dust-moted sunbeams slanted down through the dimness. From somewhere high up came a low twitter of birds.

"Kitty—kitty."

The only answer to April's call was the scrabble of tiny feet across the loft overhead. Ellen fled back to the barnyard.

"Come away from that mouse-haunted place!" she cried.

April followed her aunt outside, closing the door behind her.

"Of course Tinkerbell wouldn't answer a stranger's call," she said. "But at least I'll be able to tell Sally that we have a clue to the whereabouts of the kittens."

As soon as they returned from the village, she walked over to the Oliver house. Sally was delighted at the news.

"We'll go up to the Alder house tomorrow and comb the place until we find Tinker's hideaway."

In the small hours of the next morning April was startled awake by a sharp explosion that sounded to her like a gunshot somewhere nearby in the forest. She sat up in bed, her heart pounding heavily. Outside her window the gray woods were as still as the dawn. She clutched the covers, tense and listening. Then, from high up on Deer Hill behind the cottage, came another sound like a rifle shot. At the same time an explanation came to April. There must be a road up there, and someone's car was backfiring on the steep grade!

Laughing at her first silly notion of hearing shots in the summer woods, April snuggled down to sleep.

While Tinkerbell was eating her dinner that day, Sally and April stole away to the Alder place. Sally did a gleeful little dance step as they passed her worm sign.

"I've sold five dollars' worth of worms this week," she confided. "And this is only Tuesday. I am putting half away toward buying hybrids to improve my stock. The rest goes into a fund Kent and I have started to buy a new tractor." She sighed. "Farm machinery costs a frightful lot of money, and I don't know how Kent expects to earn his part. Papa can't pay him anything for the work he does on the farm. It's tough on Kent to have to give all his time at home. He wants to go to forestry school, but there doesn't seem to be much chance that he will ever make it."

Upon reaching the Alder place, the girls hid behind a stone wall that bordered the driveway. April found a stick and poked cautiously about in the tall grass in case snakes should be lurking there.

"We don't have poisonous snakes in Maine," Sally told her.

"I don't want to sit on *any* kind of snake," April said firmly.

"Shh!" Sally hissed, drawing her down in the grass. "Tinker could hear us talking 'way up the road. Only a bear has keener ears than a cat."

April settled herself comfortably with her back against the bole of a maple tree. In the leafy branches above her a yellow-throated warbler was chirping to its young ones, urging them to try their wings. Just as I am trying my wings away from home this summer, April thought.

She felt a prickle of guilt as she realized how little she had missed her family and Jean these last few days. She hadn't really given a thought to Crescent Beach and her friends there! I'll send them all postcards the very next time I go to the village, she vowed to herself with a rush of loyalty.

But she could not deny that she was having a much better time in Maine than she had expected.

Sally nudged her. "Here she comes!" she whispered.

April peeked cautiously over the wall.

Tinkerbell was padding along the driveway. With not the least suspicion that she was being watched by two pairs of eager eyes, she trotted to a spot where a honeysuckle vine covered a trellis at the end of the ell porch. Hooking her claws into the heavy twists of vine, she climbed paw over paw to the porch roof. Then, cleverly, she poked a forepaw at one of the shuttered windows opening on the roof. The shutter swung slightly open and Tinkerbell slipped behind it and disappeared.

"So that's it!" Sally exclaimed. "The little dickens!" She stood up and clambered over the wall. "I hope we're cats enough to climb that vine."

April looked up at the roof with inward misgivings. "Why don't we see if there's a ladder in the barn?"

She led the way to the side door of the barn and started in. Just inside the door she let out a startled cry and jumped back, bumping hard into Sally.

"Hi! What's up!" Sally stood on one foot while she used both hands to hold the toes April had stepped on.

April's face was ashen. "It's the barn. I had a spooky feeling the moment I got inside—and then I saw —s-something hanging in there—"

"Something hanging?" Sally asked in a puzzled voice as she straightened up.

April backed away from the door. "Something big, like a b-body. Honestly, it looked sinister. And it wasn't hanging there yesterday when Aunt Ellen and I were in the barn." Her eyes looked enormous. "Sally, I'm scared."

Sally looked at her a moment in silence, then she said firmly: "You're just imagining things."

She stepped past April and walked into the barn. Inside, she stopped near the door, narrowing her eyes as she peered into the vast, dim interior. April swallowed hard and then followed Sally. Standing on tiptoe, she peered over Sally's shoulder. She gasped, blinked her eyes, and looked again.

The barn was empty!

"You must have seen a shadow." In spite of her bravado, Sally sounded relieved.

"No! Something was hanging from that beam over there near the center of the barn," April persisted.

She pointed to a large beam set with hooks that had probably once held harness or farm implements.

"Let's have a closer look," Sally said.

She started to walk across the barn, but stopped in her tracks as a banshee-wailing let loose from near the place where April had seen the thing hanging.

Whoo—Hooo—Whooooo.

With a low cry April grabbed Sally's arm and pulled her out into the barnyard, slamming the door shut behind them.

"We're not going into that creepy place again, Sally Oliver!"

"It was only a barn owl," Sally protested, but she meekly followed April along the driveway back to the house.

"I am not sure it was a bird," April said grimly, looking back over her shoulder at the red barn.

Kittens or no kittens, she wished they had stayed away from the old Alder place!

"We sure are brave to let a bird scare us," Sally said in disgust. "Oh well, we probably wouldn't have found a ladder in the barn anyway."

They looked into the woodshed and found it crowded

with all the various things that collect about a country house: old jugs, a flatiron, baskets, coils of rope hanging from nails on the wall, a rusty axe, a few logs piled up. But no ladder.

"I guess it will have to be the vine after all."

Sally walked over to the trellis and shook it to test its strength; then she began to climb, using the crosspieces of the trellis for steps. In a surprisingly short time she was on the roof. Crouching there, her brown eyes dancing, she grinned down at April.

"Coming up?"

April could think of any number of things she'd rather do than climb that trellis. She glanced down unhappily at her pink dacron blouse and immaculate white linen Bermuda shorts; then she looked up at the roof, looming above her like the Matterhorn. She had never climbed a tree or even a fence in all her life; she wondered what Perry would think if he could see his "lace petticoat" sister even attempting such a thing. And Mom!

"Hurry!" Sally called impatiently.

April sighed and reached among the honeysuckle leaves and flowers to take a firm hold on the trellis.

She guessed she'd have to forget lace petticoats and find a dash of tomboy if she wanted to be friends with Sally.

Gingerly she started the climb. Leaves and tendrils poked into her eyes and mouth as she hugged the trellis tightly. Sharp, dead pieces of the vine scratched her legs, her blouse caught on a nail and tore. She struggled upward, and was almost at the top of the trellis, when the bar on which she was standing cracked ominously. April squealed and pulled herself up desperately by her hands. Sally, kneeling on the roof, leaned over the edge and grabbed her by the back of her blouse. Breathing hard, April scrambled to safety on the roof.

Kneeling beside Sally, April looked down at the ground, which seemed far away. She felt a secret thrill of pride at her own daring in having climbed to the roof, and she was a little put out with Sally for being so casual.

The roof was just a gentle slope to the windows above the porch. Sally pulled back the shutter behind which Tinkerbell had disappeared. A bottom pane of glass was missing from the twelve pane window. That explained how Tinker had entered the house, but how she had found the broken window pane to begin with was a mystery that only another cat could have understood.

The window went up easily. The girls climbed over the still and found themselves in a low-ceilinged room, furnished with an old spool bedstead stripped down to just a mattress and a pillow. Tinkerbell lay on the mattress, curled up against the pillow. Pressed against her were four dark little balls of fur. The big cat looked at the girls with half-closed amber eyes and the sound of her purring filled the room.

"Tinkerbell, you rascal!" Sally exclaimed softly.

Never before had April seen such tiny kittens as these. Tenderness welled up in her. She bent over the bed and timidly put out a finger to stroke one of the fat little creatures.

The kittens' eyes were open, but they were still unsteady on their short little legs. April and Sally sat on the edge of the bed and watched them stagger about on the mattress, tumbling and rolling as the mother cat watched them proudly. The girls let out peals of laughter at the sprawling antics of the kittens. Tinkerbell behaved indulgently toward both her children and the visitors, but when one of the kittens ventured too close to the edge of the bed, she would get up and lug it back to safety by the back of its neck.

Sally jumped to her feet. "We'd better start getting them out of here." She thought a moment, her lip caught between her teeth. "I'll get that old egg basket we saw in the woodshed. I think there's a piece of rope too."

She climbed out of the window and disappeared down the honeysuckle vine.

Left alone in the quiet house with the cat family, April began to feel uneasy. For one thing, she did not like being a housebreaker, and for another, after their experience in the barn, she had had quite enough of deserted old buildings for one day. She stared at the door that probably opened into a hall. If anything started wailing in this house, she'd be off that roof like a grasshopper!

She stood up and looked out of the window, wishing Sally would hurry. Then she wandered restlessly about the room.

Except for the stripped bed, and the gray layers of dust spread over everything, the room looked as though it might have been occupied only yesterday. It was obviously a boy's room. On a rack above the door was a small rifle and a fishing rod. Shelves built along one wall held a collection of minerals and Indian arrowheads. The top of an old secretary desk was stuffed with books.

A voracious reader herself, April could not resist pulling open the glass doors of the secretary for a closer look at the titles of the books. All of them seemed to be nature and adventure books. She pulled out one titled *The Lost World*, by A. Conan Doyle. Opening it, she saw the name "Jim Alder" scrawled across the flyleaf.

In startled delight, April stood with the book in her hand, gazing about the room. Of course this was just the sort of room one would expect of a boy who was destined to grow up to a life of adventure in far places, and a career of writing about it. Wait till she told Aunt Ellen about being in Jim Alder's room! Then her smile faded. With a guilty feeling she pushed the book back into place and closed the doors of the secretary.

Aunt Ellen would not be at all thrilled to hear that her niece had been prying about in someone else's house!

"Hi!" cried Sally's cheerful voice from the porch roof. She had a short-handled egg basket and a coil of rope.

The basket was softly cushioned with long grass. Tinker meowed a protest as the girls gently lifted her babies into the basket; she caught one by the loose skin of its neck and carried it back to the pillow. Sally promptly put the protesting kitten back in the basket.

"We won't hurt your children, Tinker," she assured the worried mother cat.

The girls crawled out on the roof with the precious basket, Tinkerbell fussing and getting under foot every inch of the way.

Sally shut the window and closed the shutter.

"I'll tell Chuck about this broken window the next time I see him."

She tied one end of the rope to the handle of the basket and lay down on her stomach to lower the basket slowly over the edge of the roof. Seeing her children vanishing into space, Tinker hurled herself onto the honeysuckle vine and clawed her way to the ground. As soon as the basket touched earth, she crammed her head and front paws into it and began to wash the kittens fiercely with her pink tongue.

"I suppose that's her way of counting them," April said, as she and Sally followed Tinkerbell down the vine.

She was so interested in the kittens that she forgot to be afraid of the climb down the trellis.

Sally took a quick glance at the sun, sinking low behind the trees.

"Yipe! I'll be late for the milking."

She snatched up the basket and sprinted down the driveway, trailed by April and Tinkerbell. The cat kept meowing anxiously to the kittens, whose little heads kept bobbing up over the edge of the basket. Sally was near the drive entrance when a small truck turned recklessly into the driveway from Deer Hill Road. She jumped wildly to one side to avoid being knocked down. Brakes shrieked as the truck ground to a stop. One of the two men on the front seat jumped out.

It was George Crawly.

6. FIRST DATE

"THAT'S NO WAY TO COME tearing in here!" Sally cried.

She was white and shaken from her near-accident.

George shot a suspicious glance from her to April. "What are you kids doing here?" he demanded.

"We could ask you the same thing," Sally snapped.

She started to walk past him, but he grabbed her basket and peered inside.

"Ho—kittens," he jeered. "Foolish girl stuff."

Indignantly Sally pulled the basket away from him.

His eyes narrowed. "Where did you find those varmints? Have you been in the—"

Kent's voice came crisply from behind the two girls. "What's it to you, George, where they've been?"

April spun around in surprise. Kent was standing close to her and Sally, scowling at George.

"You'd better be on your way, George," Kent suggested, his eyes as hard and full of light as those of a hawk.

George glared at him. "Are you nuts? We came here to—"

"I said get going!" Kent shouted. "And the next time you turn into a yard, look where you're going! You could have killed my sister."

"Aw, go jump in the lake!" George said disgustedly.

He climbed into the truck and muttered something to the driver, a dark man with a small mustache. They backed out of the driveway and rattled off up the road.

"George Crawly is up to some kind of funny business," Sally guessed, frowning after the truck. She turned to her brother with a smile. "Am I glad you told him off! But how did you get here? You didn't come by the road."

He grinned. "Heard any barn owls today?"

"Kent Oliver! It was you making that horrible noise."

He nodded. "You two sure are a couple of fraidy cats."

"But what were you doing in the barn?"

"I promised Chuck I'd sort of keep an eye on the place," he said shortly.

"Then you had better watch George Crawly."

78

"I will!"

Remembering the milking, Sally took off suddenly down the road with the basketful of kittens. Tinker trotted anxiously at her heels, and April and Kent followed close behind.

April discovered that she had to lengthen her steps considerably to keep up with Kent's long, easy strides. She put up her hand to push her curly bang off her hot forehead, and found to her dismay that there were honeysuckle leaves sticking in her hair. Suddenly she realized that she must look a mess. Furtively she made an effort to tuck her blouse neatly into her shorts. There was a long tear in one sleeve. And her once spotless shorts were smudged with dirt from the ancient trellis and the dusty room. What must Kent think of her?

She stole a glance at him and surprised him looking at her. Both of them burst out laughing because they were reminded of that first day of their meeting on the train.

"You are getting a keen tan," Kent said. "It sure is becoming."

A happy glow spread through April, because Kent's eyes were so obviously admiring. Maybe he hadn't noticed how disheveled she was. Then, on second thought, she realized that Kent was too sensible to expect a girl to look as though she had just stepped out of a beauty parlor after an adventure such as she and Sally had just had with the kittens. She swung along beside him filled with new, exhilarating confidence.

As they walked into the Oliver yard, Pete came trotting down the path to welcome his family. At the sight of the big setter, Tinkerbell let out a war whoop. Dashing ahead of Sally, she planted herself squarely in the dog's way; she had swelled up until every hair stood on end, and she looked almost as big as Pete himself. Surprise rocked the dog back on his heels. Tinkerbell shrieked again and flew at him, lashing him right and left across the nose with her claws. Pete yipped in anguish and backed up once more. Tinker went after him again, but before she could lay a claw on him, Pete tore behind a flowering quince bush and peeked out at her in honest bewilderment.

Tinkerbell minced back to convoy Sally and the kittens safely past the quince bush.

"Poor Pete," Sally said between giggles. "I don't think he would harm the kittens, but it is best not to take chances—at least Tinker seems to think so."

When the rest of the family was in the kitchen, and it was safe for him to leave the shelter of the quince, Pete stole up on the doorstone to peer in through the screen in a hurt sort of way.

Sally found a larger basket for the kittens, and lined it with a piece of soft quilt. She placed the basket in a dim corner of the kitchen. Tinker accepted these arrangements at once, jumping into the basket to wash her mewing babies, and then curling down to nurse them.

"We had better leave them alone now," Sally said.

"Tinker is purring, so I hope she'll be contented in her new nest."

She went outside to comfort the disconsolate setter.

Kent walked with April past the orchard, as far as the cottage mailbox. The little red flag was standing up on the box, to signal that the rural mailman had stopped on his rounds. April pulled the box open and found two letters for her aunt and a letter and a postcard for herself. The bulky letter was from Jean. The card had a picture in color of the familiar row of cottages at Crescent Beach; on the back was scrawled "We miss you, doll." It was signed by every one of the crowd that gathered in the store up the road for sodas and chit-chat between sailing, swimming, and tennis. April smiled over the list of signatures, then held out the card for Kent to see.

"This is Crescent Beach, where I've spent every summer I can remember, until now. Our cottage is at the end, near the rocks."

Kent peered at the picture. "Nice," he said. "But it looks a little crowded."

Miffed at his lack of enthusiasm, April pushed the card between the letters she held in her other hand.

Kent's thoughts were on something other than Crescent Beach. "I sold that big snapper to the Bear Paw Inn," he told April. "They gave me four dollars for him."

"That's an awful lot of money for an ugly old turtle."

"He won't be ugly served up as turtle soup." Kent

shifted his feet nervously. His next words came out in a rush, as if he were afraid that if he did not speak fast he would never get them out at all. "The circus is coming to Mayville next Saturday. Wouldn't you like to go?"

April nodded. "I'd love it, but I don't think Aunt Ellen would care for it. She is here to rest, you know."

"I meant would you like to go with me?"

"Oh!"

A sudden shyness made April avoid his earnest eyes. She looked down at the letters in her hands, and shuffled them nervously. Boys had seen her home from parties and school affairs, but this was the first time a boy had asked her for a date.

"I—I don't know," she stammered.

"Chuck is taking Sally to the afternoon performance. We could all ride over together. I'd like awfully for you to go," Kent urged.

April looked up at him. There was something about Kent, with his strong features and hawk-keen eyes, that made all the other boys she had ever known seem colorless and uninteresting. She remembered that Sally had confided that Kent didn't pay much attention to girls, and that he had never asked a girl for a date. How wonderful that now he should be asking her!

"I'd enjoy going with you, Kent." Her voice and manner were a little prim, because this was her very first date. "I'll ask Aunt Ellen."

George Crawly's truck rumbled along the road and passed them in a cloud of dust, headed toward the Alder place. April stared after it.

"Your friend always seems to be in a terrific hurry," she said.

"He's not my friend."

Kent turned away abruptly and tramped back in the direction of the farmhouse. April stared after him in astonishment, feeling let down and hurt because, after being so friendly a moment ago, he had now apparently forgotten her existence. She started slowly along the path to the cottage, but she had gone only a few steps when she heard Kent call.

"Wait a second!"

She swung around. Kent was striding back in her direction, as if he had just remembered something of importance. He stopped a little way off from where April waited, her face unsmiling, the green of the pine boughs overhead reflected in her cloudy eyes.

"I've got to hustle," Kent explained. "There's a chore that needs doing."

"You could at least say good-by when you leave a person," April said coldly.

"I'm sorry." Kent really did sound contrite. "You won't forget about the circus?"

He looked so anxious that April melted and a little smile played around the corners of her mouth. Kent had so much to do, so many worries and responsibilities, that it was no wonder he was absent-minded.

"I'll ask Aunt Ellen the moment I get home."

"Great!" Kent made her an elaborate bow. "Auf Wiedersehen, Miss Merriman."

"Au revoir, Mr. Oliver," she laughed.

She waved her hand and went on up the knoll.

"You tell your aunt I'll take good care of you!" Kent called after her.

April's heart was singing, and her feet were as light as a chipmunk's upon the path as she hurried on.

Ellen was sitting in a rustic chair under the pines, reading a novel. April tossed her two letters into her lap, and then threw herself down on the reddish mat of pine needles to open her own letter from Jean.

Her face grew pensive as she read the long, newsy account of all the doings at Crescent Beach, and she felt a twinge of homesickness—something she had not experienced since her first day at Deer Hill. The feeling passed, because, although she sincerely missed Jean and her other friends, she had found rich compensations for giving up her summer at the beach. If she had not come to Deer Hill she would never have gotten to know Sally and Kent, and Pete, and the kittens. And the beauty and mystery of the unspoiled woods would still be a closed book to her.

She folded Jean's letter, and then lay back with her hands clasped behind her head, so she could watch the pointed tops of the trees swaying gently against the blue sky with its slowly drifting clouds. The soughing of the pines was a soothing lullaby. Somewhere among the trees a vesper sparrow was throating its silvery spirals; from deeper in the wood a thrush answered with a note as clear as a bell.

"My, it's nice here," April murmured. "And how good it smells!"

Ellen tucked the letter she had been reading inside her book. "There's a verse of Lowell's that came to mind as I was sitting here:

> *Under the yaller-pines I house*
> *When sunshine makes 'em all sweet-scented,*
> *An' hear among their furry boughs*
> *The baskin' west-wind purr contented.*

"*I* feel like purring," April said, stretching out.

Ellen laughed. "I wish your mother could see you now. You've changed in some intangible way this summer—and the change is very becoming."

April shook her head, then she sat up, smoothing back her hair. "I guess Mom wouldn't think much of me." She looked ruefully down at her clothes. "White linen shorts are fine for the shore, but they are definitely not for climbing about old houses. And I've torn my blouse—"

She held out her arm for her aunt to see.

"I'll mend that rip so it won't show at all," Ellen promised. "What have you and Sally been up to?"

"We found Tinkerbell's kittens in a bedroom at the Alder place. We had to climb up to the roof and enter the house through a window."

Ellen looked astonished. "I'm afraid I cannot approve of that, dear. Breaking into someone's house is distinctly illegal, and could be dangerous as well."

"I know, Aunt Ellen. But Sally just had to get the kittens out of there," April pleaded. "We came away as soon as we could. And now Sally can tell Chuck about the broken window and loose shutter. It is really a good thing for the house that Tinker led us to that open shutter, so everything can be made tight before bad weather sets in."

Ellen laughed. "Perhaps. But please do not go prowling around down there any more. Did Sally get the kittens home safely?"

April nodded. "There are four of them—darlings." She clasped her knees and sat looking at her aunt with a shy smile. "Kent asked me to go to the circus with him Saturday afternoon—over at Mayville. Chuck is taking Sally, and we would all go over together. Chuck will be driving his father's car. I'd love to go."

"You may go, of course," said her aunt. "I am sure your parents would approve of both Kent and Chuck.

The only condition is that you be home, off the road, before dark."

"It's my first date," April confided bashfully.

Ellen looked at her tenderly. "You will have a wonderful time." A faraway look with a hint of sadness came into her blue eyes. "I remember my first date. It was a school dance, and I wore my first formal—"

Through words her parents had let drop in her hearing, April knew something about her aunt's sad love story; Ellen had become engaged to her girlhood sweetheart, and then he had been killed in World War II. April suspected that her mother worried about her pretty sister-in-law, because now romance seemed only a thing of the past to Ellen.

Ellen was smiling again. "I have some other good news for you, April. Mrs. Oliver and I have been talking over the matter of that old cabin by the pond, and we have decided to let you and Sally have your week of camping down there."

"Oh! That's just the greatest, Aunt Ellen!"

But the date with Kent shone much closer than the camping trip, and it was that which occupied most of April's thoughts until Saturday.

Saturday dawned clear and sunny, a perfect circus day. April washed her hair and set the front in curls. She used Ellen's traveling iron to press her dress, a wide-skirted green cotton satin, printed with a scattering of pink and white daisies. She fastened her pony tail with a cluster of pink daisies. Her shoes were flat-heeled green pumps.

She was in a happy glow as she walked down the path with Kent, who was spruced up in slacks and a new, plaid sports shirt.

"My, that's a pretty dress!" Sally greeted April.

She was sitting beside Chuck in the front seat of the dark red car. Kent opened the rear door for April.

"You look lovely, Sally," April returned the compliment.

It was true, because Sally would have looked good in anything. Today she wore a buttercup-yellow cotton dress with a perky white collar, but the dress was old and had the look of many tubbings behind it. At home April would have been proud to be the best-dressed girl in the party, but here, surprisingly, she did not feel good about having on a prettier dress than Sally.

Why, she thought to herself, I must like Sally Oliver better than any girl I ever knew—better than Jean even, and that's an awful lot!

Chuck glanced from one girl to the other with an admiring grin.

"You two look like a buttercup and daisy field."

April hoped Kent might say something nice about her appearance, but he sat beside her in moody silence almost all the way to Mayville.

"Kent is sulking because we're going to camp at the cabin," Sally said over her shoulder. "Mama told him this morning."

"It's too lonely at that old cabin for a couple of girls by themselves," Kent muttered.

"He even tried to persuade Mama not to let me go," Sally laughed. She turned around to give her brother a merry glance. "Stop acting like an old granny, Kent! We used to go camping alone when you were only twelve and I was eleven."

"That was different," Kent said shortly.

"When are you chicks planning to be at the cabin?" Chuck asked.

He was a good driver and kept his eyes carefully on the road ahead, even while he was talking.

"Week after next," Sally told him.

He nodded. "Aw, what's to worry about, Kent? The girls will be okay."

"Yeah. I suppose so."

Kent managed a grin and seemed to be in a more cheerful mood during the remainder of the drive. As he helped April out of the car at the circus parking lot, he whistled, as if he were seeing her for the first time that afternoon.

"Sure is a sharp outfit, Miss Merriman."

She laughed up at him. "Thank you, Mr. Oliver."

The circus was a small, two-ring affair, but it was

glamorous to the four young people. They thrilled to the daring of the aerial performers and the high wire artists, and laughed themselves weak over the antics of the clowns. The lion trainer's valor had them sitting tensely on the edges of their chairs. The bareback riders brought gasps of admiration. In between times they put away astonishing amounts of hot dogs, peanuts, and soft drinks.

They were starry-eyed at the end of the performance, as they left the Big Top to stroll along the garish little midway, each couple hand-in-hand. At the shooting gallery the boys stopped to show how they could shoot down the clay ducks in the moving line at the back of the booth. Kent's skill with the rifle brought admiring comments from the crowd.

"Nice going, feller," a voice rasped approvingly.

It was George Crawly. At the sight of him Kent's sullen mood returned. He laid the rifle down and refused to fire it again, although the owner of the gallery offered to let him shoot for nothing in order to draw a crowd.

"We don't often see such shooting, young feller," the man urged.

Kent shook his head and turned to George. "I want to talk to you, Crawly."

He pushed George into the narrow space between two sideshow tents. Chuck excused himself to the girls and followed Kent. April and Sally lingered uncomfortably at a little distance.

"Now what in the world can Kent have to say to George Crawly that is so important?" Sally said in the crossest voice April had ever heard her use.

The boys seemed to be having a hot argument, George against the other two. In spite of the chatter and laughter of the people thronging the midway, the girls caught a word now and then.

"Aw, you're just stalling," George growled, after Kent had obviously put some sort of proposition to him.

Kent turned away. "Take it or leave it—and if you want to leave it, that's okay by me," he flung over his shoulder.

George grabbed his arm. "No need to get sore, Kent. We've got a contract and I expect you to keep your part of it."

Kent brushed him off, but George kept right on talking. Their voices sank to a murmur. "Why not try the other side?" Chuck suggested.

"It's not as accessible—and we've got a good set-up where we are," George said angrily.

But when Kent started away again, George agreed hastily to whatever it was the others wanted. "Okay, okay," he mumbled. "But the boss won't like this."

"Tough on him," Chuck said cheerfully.

Whistling, he joined the two girls. Kent followed, scowling. George slouched off by himself.

Puzzled, April looked after George. What was going on with him and Kent and Chuck? The boys seemed to dislike young Crawly almost as much as Sally did, yet it was plain that he and they were involved in some sort of mysterious business together. And, whatever this business was, the mere thought of it seemed to be enough to make Kent as grouchy as a bear.

7. A SHOT IN THE NIGHT

APRIL SAW LITTLE OF SALLY and Kent during the
days following their circus jaunt. She felt she should
spend most of her time with her aunt to make up for
the week she would be away at the cabin by the pond.
This did not involve a sacrifice, however, for Ellen was a
delightful companion, full of vim and merriment now
that she was almost recovered from her long illness.

They explored the woods around their cottage, and
one day they took a picnic lunch and climbed to the top
of Deer Hill. They ate their sandwiches and oranges beneath wind-scrubbed cedars and spruce trees on the

granite backbone of the hill, where long scars on the rock bore witness to the glacier that had ground over the land thousands of years gone by. In the far distance glimmered the peaks of the White Mountains over in New Hampshire. Close at hand, Mik-Chik Pond, a jewel of lapis-lazuli, nestled deep under the ridge that was Deer Hill. Across the pond another wooded ridge divided Mik-Chik from a larger lake that sparkled away into the blue distance.

"It's a view to lift one's heart to God in praise," Ellen murmured, breathing deep of the bracing air with its aromatic scents of sun-warmed conifers.

April sprawled on a flat boulder, soaking up the sunshine. The glimpse of Mik-Chik Pond below them had set her to wondering anew why Kent had made her and Sally promise to keep away from the pond all this week. Sally had confided that Kent himself walked down there every day between chores.

"I think he is fixing some sort of a surprise to make up for his surliness when he first learned of our camping project," Sally said to April, one morning when she brought Ellen's milk, butter, and fresh eggs over to the cottage. "But I hope he stays away from the cabin; we want to tidy that up ourselves."

On a day of sunny blue skies and high, gently drifting cumulus clouds, Ellen took April and Sally on a long drive to Pemaquid Point. This was April's first glimpse of the rugged Maine seacoast. The long fingers of granite, black to the tideline with pointed spruce, reaching out into the tumultuous, beryl-green water, and the pound, surge, and far-flung diamond spray of the great waves upon the rocky off-shore ledges made a scene of splendor she would remember and treasure forever.

After a few hours of leisurely exploration, Ellen and the two girls had a seafood dinner at a lobster wharf on one of the deep, spruce-fringed inlets that penetrated the coast. It was late afternoon when Ellen again pointed the car toward Bear Paw. Sunset and approaching dusk found them driving along a narrow road with many turns, and with woods crowding close on both sides. Suddenly a hulking animal on legs like stilts strode out of the woods and stopped in the middle of the road, facing the car. Ellen put on the brake so hard that April thought they were all three going to crash through the windshield. She clutched Sally, and Sally grabbed her just as tightly. All of them stared in awe and terror at the gigantic moose blocking the road.

"Don't move or make a sound!" Sally warned in a whisper. "Maybe he'll ignore us."

April's heart was pounding. Ever since coming to Maine, the dread of meeting a moose in the woods had persisted at the back of her mind; now that fear had become a reality, and it was quite as alarming as she had imagined it would be.

Even her imagination, boosted by pictures she had seen, had not prepared her for a creature so enormous.

The moose was bigger than a horse, and the spreading crown of his palmated antlers, still in velvet, seemed to fill the road from side to side. April went cold with the thought that, if he chose to charge the car, he would probably wreck it, and its occupants too.

The moose stood with his head slightly lowered as he studied the car with his gleaming little eyes. His nostrils dilated and he shook his antlers, as if he did not like the evil smell or shining look of the strange animal squatting in the road. He took a majestic step closer.

"He's going to charge at us!" Ellen exclaimed through dry lips. "Dear Heaven, what shall we do?"

As if by instinct, her hand descended on the auto horn and pressed hard. The blast that ripped through the gathering twilight set the astonished moose back on his haunches. He snorted and began to paw the ground with one front hoof.

"Now you've done it!" Sally groaned. "He probably thinks we're some sort of animal challenging him to battle. Yell, everyone!" she commanded. "Sing!"

She launched into *Home on the Range* at the top of her lungs. In a shaky voice April joined in with *Oh Hartford High, of Thee I sing*. Ellen whooped and sounded the horn frantically, again and again.

The queer medley of sound seemed to baffle the moose. He kept his antlers lowered toward the bellowing squat thing, ready to charge if the other showed fight, but the desire to start a fight seemed to have gone out of him. Suddenly he turned, trotted into the woods, and disappeared among the shadowy trees.

"Whee!" April went limp against the seat. "I thought it was curtains for all of us—including Aunt Ellen's new car."

Ellen started the car with frenzied haste. "Let's get away from here before he decides to come back."

"We were lucky."

Sally turned her head to look back through the rear window. The lonely road remained empty of life. As the car rounded a turn, Sally gave a sigh of relief and faced front again.

"Yes, we were lucky all right," she repeated. "If it had been autumn, and that big fellow's antlers had been hardened enough to fight with, we probably would not have gotten off without a smashed car at least. But in midsummer antlers are still tender. Mr. Moose obviously did not care to risk injuring his in battle with a crazy-voiced critter like this car." She chuckled. "He sure did look surprised when we began to serenade him."

Ellen was still pale from the fright of the meeting. "Do many motorists encounter moose on Maine roads?" she asked.

"Every so often you hear of a case," said Sally. "They say the safest thing to do is to stop the car and keep still until the moose goes away. Sometimes they just seem curious; once in a while, however, the sight of a moving car seems to enrage them. I once heard of a car being turned over by a furious moose. Yet Papa once met a big fellow face to face in the woods and nothing happened—each of them went his own way in peace."

April was listening with the avid interest that any talk of wildlife awakened in her. Ellen switched on the headlights. She too, as she guided the car along the winding road, was keenly alert to what Sally was saying.

"You never know what a wild animal will do," Sally went on. "Some moose, and buck deer, are evil-tempered and spoiling for a fight, but there are some that seem to have the inclination to be friendly. A few weeks ago two moose came out of the woods and grazed peacefully on Monmouth green for hours. People went close enough to take snapshots. No one got hurt."

Remembering the huge dark body and the regal spread of antlers, April decided that she would as lief not meet any more moose, even well-disposed ones. But today's encounter would be something exciting to write about to Perry.

On her next trip to Bear Paw, April bought a pair of blue jeans at the general store. She had always considered jeans unbecoming and unfeminine and had never before owned a pair, but now Sally and she were planning to clean up the old cabin before they moved in, and she could not picture herself doing that messy job in any of her smart summer outfits.

Ellen highly approved of the purchase.

"You'll find jeans comfortable and practical for the woods," she said. "Safe around open fires too."

Wearing her new jeans and oldest blouse, and with the red bathing suit she had bought to wear at Crescent Beach rolled in a towel under her arm, April went over to the farmhouse the next day to help Sally carry window screening and some other things that would be needed at the cabin.

In the kitchen Pete was sprawled on the floor near the kitten basket, and Tinkerbell was sitting complacently on a nearby window sill, washing her face while she kept watchful eyes on her offspring. The kittens were tumbling in and out of their basket, scuffling and boxing in soft-footed glee. Pete's tongue curled out in a grin as he watched them with bright eyes.

"Pete and Tinkerbell seem to have reached some sort of understanding about the kittens," Sally said. "He must have convinced her that he means them well. He's crazy about them. Thinks he's their uncle."

One of the kittens started out into the center of the room on an exploring jaunt. Suddenly his legs spread wide and he sprawled on his nose with a tiny "Meow!" of astonishment. With a laugh April scooped him up in her two hands. "Precious," she murmured, holding the fluffy mite against her cheek.

Why hadn't she discovered long ago how sweet a kitten could be!

Pete watched anxiously until April put the kitten

back on the floor, then he stood up and with his black nose urged the fat, furry little thing tenderly back toward the safety of the basket. Usually eager for a walk, the setter did not even turn his head when Sally opened the kitchen door and the two girls went outside.

As Sally and April were crossing the yard, an automobile stopped on the road opposite the worm sign.

"Miss, can you supply me with about three dozen worms?" the driver called.

"It will take only a minute," Sally told April.

A second fisherman got out of the car and followed Sally to the woodshed. April trailed behind them. It still seemed incredible to her that Sally could make money out of earthworms.

Sally took a pronged stick and turned over the soil in one of the butter tubs, picking up the lively red worms as they appeared, and dropping them into an empty tin can. April pursed her lips in distaste. At his request, Sally put another three dozen worms into a can for the other fisherman.

"They're good worms, miss, lively and juicy." The man all but smacked his lips over them. "Many's the old bass who will turn up his snout at a fancy lure to go for worms like these."

"Good worms are hard to find," his friend added, digging into his pocket for some change. "We got some over near Lake Androscoggin, but they were so feeble they passed out on us before we reached the lake."

Sally smiled at them with her warm brown eyes. "These are hand-raised worms." She told the fishermen how she had sent to Washington for a pamphlet on worm culture. "I'm just starting, but I mean to build it into a full-sized business," she confided.

"We'll spread the word that first-class worms can be bought on Deer Hill Road," the men promised as they drove away.

Sally and April started down the tote road, lugging tools, wire screening, an old broom, rags, and a scrub pail.

"Kent says he will look after my customers while I'm away that week," Sally said. "I'm hoping he will become interested enough in the work to go partners with me."

"Could you make enough for it to be worth Kent's time?" April asked.

Sally paused to settle the roll of screening more firmly on her shoulder. "We could sell worms by mail to zoos and gardeners, and to fish breeders. It could be a year-round, thriving business. I put my pamphlet on worm culture in Kent's room and I hope he'll read it and realize all the possibilities for himself." She gave a deep discouraged sigh. "But Kent seems so moody and grouchy lately! He doesn't want to talk about anything. I know he is awfully worried about Papa's health and getting things done on the farm, but something else must be troubling him too. It's queer—Kent was never one to have secrets."

"You told me that Kent wants to go to forestry school," April reminded her. "With all the financial worries your family has, and all the work piling up at home, he probably feels that he will have to give up that dream. No wonder he's moody!"

"I guess you're right," Sally nodded. "Kent is probably looking forward to a lifetime of trying to scratch a living for the family from our sadly run-down farm." Her winsome face turned pensive. "I want to go to teachers' college, but, if I make it, earthworms will have to pay the bill."

As they walked down the tote road, deeper and deeper into the forest, Sally seemed to shrug the Oliver family troubles off her shoulders. She was in her usual bouncing spirits by the time they reached the pond which was sparkling and dancing in its setting of green hills. They paused on the wharf at the foot of the road.

"Oh!" Sally cried happily. "What do I see!"

Both girls threw down their burdens and raced out to the wharf, to stare entranced at the rowboat that was bobbing on the end of a rope. The boat was tubby, but seaworthy and neat; it was painted white and the name "April-May" was lettered in green on its bow.

"My doll of a brother has fixed up that old derelict boat for us—and what a swell job he's made of it. There's not a drop of water in the old tub." Sally got down and peered under the wharf. "And the oars are cached away under here. Oh, dear Kent! I could hug him!"

"Even if he is an old grouch sometimes," smiled April.

"He's really a wonderful brother. This explains why he wanted us to stay away from the pond. 'April-May,'" Sally exclaimed. "April for you, and May, my birth month, for me. What fun we'll have exploring the pond in our boat!"

Chattering gaily, they followed the trail to the old cabin beneath its guardian pines.

"There is an air of enchantment about this cabin," April said dreamily. "As if it had been waiting years and years for us to come and live in it. Maybe it was invisible to everyone from the day Jim Alder went away until last winter, when you came along and broke the spell. It was just waiting for us."

"It's nice to think so," Sally agreed.

She stopped a short distance from the cabin to study the fieldstone chimney that rose above the low roof. "I hope that chimney is in good condition. I'm going up there and drop a stone into it to clean it out."

"Let's open the windows first and air the room," April suggested.

The heavy, solid wooden blinds were fastened over the windows with pegs; the girls soon had them pulled back against the log walls, and the door propped wide open.

"That's better," April said, as the clean breezes began

to circulate through the stale-smelling cabin. "Now to sweep all the trash into the fireplace and burn it."

"Not until we're sure the chimney isn't blocked."

Sally went outside and searched about for a brick-shaped rock. She found one of the right size and shape on the beach, and then proceeded to tie a length of clothesline around it. She stepped up on the stump of a large tree, growing close to the cabin, and pulled herself onto the low roof. Cautiously she felt her way over the hand-rived cedar shingles to the chimney.

"This roof seems firm, thank goodness!" she reported to April on the ground.

She peered into the chimney.

"There used to be a piece of wire stretched across the chimney top," she called, "but it's all rusted away. That explains how the squirrels got into the cabin."

Slowly she lowered the stone into the chimney, swinging it around to dislodge soot and the accumulated debris of years. When she was satisfied that the chimney was as clean as she could get it, she dropped to the ground.

"Now let's see how it draws."

They swept the leaves and other litter from the bunks and floor, brushed it into the fireplace, and put a match to the pile. After a moment the fire flared up brightly. The draft whirled the smoke smoothly up the chimney.

"This is our day!" Sally caroled. "Everything is going like a song."

104

Laughing, they joined hands and capered about the room, then each one flew at her separate tasks.

Sally was handy with tools, so it was she who set about screening the cabin windows. Inside the cabin, April used the broom vigorously on the walls and floor. Then she lugged pail after pail of water from the pond. She went down on her knees to scrub the floor and stone hearth. Humming and singing under her breath, she gave the bunks a thorough cleaning. Finally she scoured the dish shelves and the thick wooden slab that formed the mantel over the fireplace.

Sally was whistling gaily as her wire cutters snipped away and her hammer went tack-tack-tack. Squirrels watched from the high branches of the surrounding trees, chipmunks whisked across the clearing and peered out shyly from behind roots and rocks. Bluejays swooped on brilliant wings and screamed raucously from the treetops, warning all the creatures in the forest that there were strange doings at the old cabin by the pond.

April hung her scrubbing rags on the edges of the bunks to dry, and stood off to admire the clean-smelling results of her toil. Sally slid off the roof, where she had fitted a new wire screen over the top of the chimney. She carefully inspected the work she had done on the windows, tapped the frames here and there, and finally threw down her hammer.

"I defy flies or 'skeeters to get through those screens!"

She joined April inside the cabin. "Golly, pard, you've done a super job in here!" Then, as she looked at April, she burst out laughing. "You look as though you've been cleaning out a coal bin."

April glanced ruefully down at her grimy, soot-blackened clothes. "My new jeans!"

"The dirt will come out in the wash," said Sally. "But how about a swim to soak the grime off *us?*"

They made a speedy change into their bathing suits and soon were diving off a big rock near the cabin, into a deep, spring-fed pool. April came up gasping and went into a vigorous crawl in an attempt to drive some warmth into her numbed body. Until today even Sally had not felt that the pond was warm enough for swimming, and this was April's first dip in the tingling water. The sun was golden, however, and the air, spiced with the scent of sun-drenched fir and hemlock, was balmy in the mid-afternoon heat.

Suddenly remembering the huge snapping turtle, April kept a nervous lookout for any of its relatives that might be lurking about. The water was so clear that little fish could plainly be seen swimming in its depths; every stone and pebble on the sandy bottom of the pond stood out sharply.

The only turtles in view were a row of gay little Painted Turtles, sunning themselves on a half-submerged log further along the pond shore. With their red spotted shells and yellow striped legs, they were in pleasant contrast to their ugly, big cousin, the snapping turtle.

"Snapping turtles shun sunshine and love mud," Sally assured April. "You are more likely to find one at the cove by the wharf, hiding under the lily leaves and ready to pounce on any prey that comes along."

The girls swam about until they tired, and then crawled out of the water to sun themselves on the big rock. Sally lay on her stomach, grinning at the Painted Turtles on their log. The turtles ranged in size from a baby shaped like a silver dollar to full-grown, six-inch oldsters. All of them had their heads stretched out in the lovely sunshine and there was an air of contentment and well-being about them.

"The Indians named Mik-Chik Pond after those little sun turtles," said Sally. "They are cheery critters to have around. I caught one last spring, when it was still sort of groggy from hibernation at the bottom of the pond. I took it home and tried to make a pet of it, but it pined in captivity and refused to eat. Finally I brought it back to the pond."

"Maybe one of those fellows over there is your turtle," said April. "Isn't that little one sort of nodding its head at you?"

Sally laughed. "It's nodding its head at the insects dancing on the water—my turtle didn't like me well enough to want to renew our acquaintance." She stood up with a little sigh. "Time to go home and tend to the chores. The cows will bellow their heads off if I'm late."

"Who will do the milking while you're away?" April asked, as they were getting dressed in the cabin.

"My good brother offered to take care of it for me. Kent really is the best!"

They rolled their damp bathing suits up in their towels, then closed and fastened the cabin door and the window blinds. As they walked across the clearing, April looked back. The cabin under the pines seemed to be dreaming with its eyes closed, waiting for Sally and her to come back again.

On the weekly trip to the village supermarket, April took along a list of supplies she was to furnish for the larder of the cabin. She used her own money to buy the things on the list, but Ellen was generous with extras. The result was a huge carton stuffed with canned beans, canned ham, tomato juice, soup, prepared cocoa, pancake and biscuit mixes, bacon, fresh and canned fruit, candy bars, and other items. April shook her head over the load.

"It doesn't seem possible that two people could use up all this in a week. And Sally's list is just as long!"

Perishables were stored in the cottage refrigerator. The rest of the supplies were left in the carton to be pulled down the tote road on a travois Sally had rigged from two clothes poles and some ancient deerskins she had found in their barn. April and Sally made another trip to the cabin Saturday afternoon with a load of canned and packaged food, soap, blankets, and a pile of old outdoor magazines found in the Olivers' attic.

"They'll come in handy if we have a rainy day," Sally said, balancing an old iron kettle on top of the magazines. "Some of the stories look keen."

Today, when they opened the cabin door, the room greeted them with a scrubbed, inviting look. Happily they unloaded the travois and carried their things inside.

"I'm glad you brought red blankets, Sally, because they give our room a needed touch of color," April said, tumbling the blankets onto the bunks.

Sally stacked the magazines on one shelf, odds and ends of dishes and cooking pots on another. Cans and packages of food made a brave showing on a third shelf. At the village general store April had bought a red-and-white checkered oilcloth to cover the crude table. After she had smoothed the cloth on, Sally placed a brightly polished lantern in the center. Each girl had brought a flashlight to hang at the head of her bunk. A coke bottle with a candle stuck in it adorned the mantelpiece.

At the very bottom of the travois load was a row of big logs from the Oliver woodpile. Sally had also brought a hatchet for chopping smaller wood.

"I'll bring some more logs the next time we come," she said, as she and April stacked the wood beside the cabin door. "We'll need a fire every night, as well as for daytime cooking."

April nodded. No matter how hot and sunny the days, as soon as the sun set here in Maine, the air grew cool.

They gathered a quantity of dry birch bark from fallen trees and a basket of pine cones to be used for kindling; then they scoured the woods near the cabin collecting sizable pieces of dead wood. Sally used her hatchet skillfully, to chop the branches into usable lengths. After they had built up a substantial woodpile, they laid a fire in the fireplace, ready to be touched off the day they moved into the cabin.

"The next time we come it will be to stay!"

The girls smiled at each other as though it were almost too wonderful to believe.

That night in her bed at Deer Hill Cottage, it seemed as if April had only just closed her eyes when she was rudely awakened by what sounded like gunfire in the woods, just as on that other night. This time the sound seemed to come from somewhere near the pond. She jerked to a sitting position and waited breathlessly to see if there would be another shot. None came. Instead, an unnatural stillness hung over the woods, as though the sound of that shot in the darkness had silenced all the voices of the wilderness in fear.

Stiffly April settled back on her pillow.

This time she was *sure* it had been a shot! But who

would be out shooting at night, and what were they shooting at? The hunting season was closed, she knew.

She thought about Monday night when she and Sally would be down at the cabin in the lonely darkness. What if someone should start shooting then! A cold wave of misgiving washed over her.

Maybe Kent was right—maybe it *was* too dangerous for two girls to camp in the woods by themselves.

But whoever was down there shooting certainly was not gunning for girls!

The idea made her giggle. She pulled the covers up around her and listened anxiously to hear if her aunt was stirring. There was no sound from the other bedroom, so evidently the shot had not awakened her. That was good. For if Ellen should suspect that there was shooting in the woods, it wouldn't take her a minute to put the kibosh on the camping expedition.

And maybe it wasn't shooting after all, April consoled herself drowsily. Maybe it was just her—imagination.

8. THE STRANGER

SALLY KNOCKED AT THE cottage door soon after breakfast Monday morning.

"Ready?" she called, her face as sparkling-fresh as if it had been washed in dew.

"All ready." April smiled at her as she held the door wide.

April had on green corduroy Bermuda shorts, a white blouse, and a cocoa-colored cashmere sweater.

Sally was wearing new jeans, moccasins, and a candy-striped blouse under her red sweater.

April had made a roll of towels, her slicker, jeans,

extra blouse and underwear, pajamas, and bathing suit. Her comb, toothbrush, and toiletries were tucked inside the roll. She placed it on the travois beside Sally's slicker roll. Heaped up at the front of the travois were Sally's provisions: fresh corn and tomatoes that had been picked from the garden that morning, a stone crock of butter, a basket of eggs, homemade bread, and sugar cookies.

"We won't go hungry," April said with a laugh.

To the load she added a carton containing bacon and frankfurters, a steak Ellen had contributed for their first meal in camp, and some brownies she had baked herself.

Taking turns, they dragged the heavy travois along the path and down the shady tote road. Ellen accompanied them in order to see the cabin and to get its exact location. This was the first time she had walked beyond the end of the tote road. She exclaimed with pleasure when she saw the picturesque log cabin.

"It's delightful! I declare, girls, I'm tempted to join you for the week."

April and Sally exchanged alarmed glances.

Ellen laughed ruefully. "Don't worry. Of course you want to be entirely free of stuffy old folks. This is your week and I'll not trespass." Her lovely face became grave. "I do not have to warn you about being careful with fire, so I'll ask only that neither of you go swimming alone, or swim too far from shore. Or take the boat out in rough weather."

"We'll be careful," April promised.

"For the rest," Ellen added with a smile, "use your common sense—and have a wonderful time."

"I'll walk back a way with you," April offered, when her aunt was ready to leave.

She was anxious to be at the cabin to help Sally unpack, so she accompanied Ellen only as far as the wharf, where the "April-May" bobbed invitingly on its skillfully tied rope.

"I'll be happy to have you back at Deer Hill Cottage a week from now," Ellen said as she kissed her niece good-by.

Her eyes mirrored the blue of the sunlit pond and the walk had brought a glow of roses to her cheeks. April looked at her in surprised admiration, as if she had never really seen how pretty her aunt was before. Why, she thought to herself, in that gay circle skirt and keen boy shirt, Aunt Ellen seems scarcely older than Sally!

She stood watching until Ellen's graceful figure was lost to sight up the green tunnel of the tote road, then she swung around to go back to the cabin.

"Oh!" she cried, startled.

A strange man was standing close behind her, but he was not looking at her; he was staring up the tote road as though he too had been watching Ellen. After a moment his eyes shifted to April.

"Hello," he said with a friendly smile.

His dark eyes, set in a deeply tanned face, were sharp and alert looking. His thick hair was black, and so was the little mustache that sat jauntily on his upper lip. He wore shabby slacks and loafers, and a green flannel shirt that was obviously far from new.

April had a sudden feeling that she had seen this stranger somewhere before, but then she told herself that the idea was ridiculous. With a stab of uneasiness she wondered who he was and what he was doing at Mik-Chik Pond. It was a good thing her aunt had not seen him. Never, never would Ellen have gone away and left her and Sally at the cabin with a strange man prowling the woods.

"Was that your sister?" the stranger asked.

"No. My aunt."

As soon as she had answered him, April wanted to bite her tongue. He had no business to ask questions—and she should have ignored him!

She hurried past him and started along the trail to the cabin, but at the first turn she could not resist glancing back. The stranger was still standing there. He grinned at her and lifted a hand in farewell. April jerked her eyes forward and sped on along the trail, her cheeks burning.

Sally was not at the cabin, but the sound of a hatchet

led April into the woods. She found Sally cutting hemlock boughs for their beds. They hauled the boughs back to the cabin and stripped off the tips. Piled lightly in the bunks with tips overlapping, the hemlock made springy mattresses. The girls stuffed their pillow slips with the very softest, new hemlock tips.

While they worked April told Sally about the stranger.

"He must be a tourist who spied the entrance to the tote road and decided to do a little exploring," April guessed. "It sure was a shock to turn around and find him standing there, as if he had materialized out of thin air. He certainly was nowhere in sight when Aunt Ellen and I were saying good-by."

"Well let's hope that Mr. Tourist is on his way by now," Sally said, as she tucked the bottom blanket over the hemlock in her bunk. "We don't want any strangers nosing about our camp."

They made a fire of apple logs because Sally said they were tops for fireplace cooking. When the hot coals heaped up in the fireplace, they wrapped well-scrubbed potatoes in aluminum foil and buried them in the coals. While the potatoes were baking, the girls went for a swim.

After the first breathless plunge was behind her, April enjoyed the exhilarating water. She and Sally took turns diving off the big rock. They swam about and raced each other until they were tired. After they had climbed out and were sunning themselves on the rock, April looked for the Painted Turtles. Heads out, they were basking in a row on the log, as on the day of her first swim in the pond. She waved a friendly hand at them before she stretched out on the rock, chuckling to herself.

Who would have dreamed that she would enjoy being neighbor to a parcel of turtles!

"Tomorrow, let's row out and explore the island," said Sally. "We'll take a lunch and picnic over there."

April propped herself on one elbow and squinted her eyes against the sun-sparkles on the water as she peered at the small island that floated halfway between them and the opposite shore.

"Chuck says Indians used to camp there in the old days, when they fished Mik-Chik Pond. I've been crazy to get a closer view of the island ever since we came to Deer Hill. Now, thanks to Kent, we've got a boat." Sally sat up. "Let's test those potatoes. I'm starving!"

They broiled the thick steak over glowing coals. The potatoes came out of their jackets smoking hot and mealy white. Ears of sweet corn were steamed to milky tenderness in a three-legged iron kettle, set among the red coals.

"Oh, oh!" April groaned, as she sat across the table from Sally. "I never ate as much as this before in my life."

"It's the air," said Sally, buttering an ear of corn. "This steak is seasoned with essence of balsam."

"And besides, we're never this hungry at home," said April.

They washed the dishes in the pond, scouring them with sand; then they stacked them on the big rock and rinsed them with boiling water from the fireplace kettle. The fireplace lacked a crane, but Sally had brought two ancient iron trivets from the seemingly inexhaustible treasure in the farmhouse attic; these were used to support the cooking pot and frying pan when they were in use in the fireplace.

After the dishes were stored away on the shelf, the girls started out with a glass gallon jug to fetch drinking water from the spring that trickled beneath a granite ledge a short way back in the woods. Near the spring they discovered a game trail with a spattering of deer tracks along it. They followed the trail and discovered that it came out at the lily-spangled cove near the end of the tote road.

"The deer must use this trail to get from the mountain to the pond," said Sally. "If we came over here before sunrise tomorrow I bet we'd surprise them. Deer love waterlilies for breakfast."

By the time they returned to the cabin, the sun had slid behind the shadowy, pine-serrated ridge across the pond, leaving behind it a glow like ashes of roses to wash across the sky. The girls had not done half the things they had planned for this first day in camp, but the whole week stretched before them with every hour for their own. Right now it was good just to sit on the big rock by the pool and watch the first stars wink back from the still water, while the woods darkened all around.

Ha-ooo. Ha—oo—ooo.

The high clear call shattered the silence that hung above the pond. It was followed by bursts of shaky laughter that ran up and down the scale.

"What on earth!" April sprang to her feet, her heart pounding. "There must be a crazy person loose!"

"It's only the loons," Sally said calmly.

"Loons?"

"Birds, somewhat like ducks—only bigger. There's a pair of them living on this pond."

April still looked worried. It was hard to believe that any bird could have made those sounds.

Out on the pond the voices rose and fell in shaky titters.

Sally laughed. "They do sound real crazy. Maybe you'll get a glimpse of them tomorrow; they're really the most interesting birds around here. Ouch!" she cried, slapping at her cheek.

Full dusk had brought clouds of buzzing, biting insects. The girls sprinted for the cabin, swatting at their arms and legs as they ran.

"I hope those screens are tight," April gasped, clawing at her back.

119

The screens were tight. Sally had done a good job on them.

As the night grew darker, a cool breeze blew up to whisper in the pines. The girls closed the blinds partway over the windows, and lit a fire on the hearth. April made cocoa while Sally toasted sandwiches for supper. Afterwards they were too tired for anything but bed.

Sally fell asleep the moment she laid her head on her hemlock-stuffed pillow.

Outside, the night was velvety-black and murmurous. Somewhere on the pond the loons were talking in low, sleepy voices. Loneliness closed about the little cabin beneath the pines. April had the feeling that she and Sally were about a thousand miles away from any other dwelling. She lay wide-eyed in her bunk, wondering what she would do if a bear should suddenly push its nose against one of the window screens. She quivered as she thought she heard a twig snap near the cabin; then she lay tense, listening with all her might. Would a moose try to batter in a cabin door if it sensed that humans were inside?

Across the cabin Sally was breathing sweetly and evenly. April knew that she herself would not be able to close her eyes all night. One of them must keep awake, in case something happened!

She turned on her side to watch the red embers glow in the fireplace. A warm fragrance rose from the hemlock crushed beneath her blanket . . . the wind was purring in the pines . . .

A hand was on April's shoulder, shaking her gently. "Get up," Sally was urging. "It's almost light."

With sweaters bundled over their pajamas and their bare feet in moccasins, they hurried through the chilly, ghostly gray woods to the lily cove. After their stealthy approach, it was a terrific disappointment to find the cove empty. But the deer had been there! In the coarse sand along the beach were big heart-shaped prints and dainty narrow ones.

"We'll have to come while it's still dark if we want to surprise them," said Sally. She stood up from examining the deer tracks and looked at April. "Have you ever heard of jacklight hunting?"

April shook her head. She was staring down ruefully at the fairy tracks of a fawn.

"Jacklighting is illegal," Sally explained. "Hunters go into the woods at night with powerful flashlights. They wait beside a deer trail until the deer come out to feed, usually just before sun-up. A light will attract a deer as surely as it does a moth. When deer see a beam of light shining in the woods, they'll walk toward it, or, if it happens to focus directly on them, they'll stand still, as if they were stunned, and then the hunters can shoot them easily."

April's lips parted in horror at this vivid description.

"Jackers are a bad lot," Sally continued. "They pay a

big fine and maybe go to jail if they're caught. But if their lights will attract deer, ours will too. We'll get up about three o'clock tomorrow and follow this deer trail toward the wood road that crosses the tote road halfway up the hill. We'll probably meet the deer coming down from the ridge to breakfast at the pond."

"But—" April thought of the size of the buck they had seen swimming the pond. "What if the deer get mad when they walk up to the light and find *us* there?"

"Oh, before they get too close, we'll laugh or sing, or do something else to scare 'em off, as we did the moose," Sally said recklessly.

That morning, over their breakfast pancakes and rashers of crisp bacon, the girls planned a cruise on the "April-May." They put up a lunch so they could picnic on the island.

The rowboat was rather tubby, but it handled well. Kent had caulked the seams before he painted it and the girls found that they did not need the can they had brought along for bailing. April took first turn at the oars. She rowed along the shore so they could have a look at their cabin from the water, then headed for the island. The row was longer than it had looked from shore, and she was glad to pull between the two big rocks that marked the entrance to a tiny landing beach on the island. It was thrilling to think that they were stepping ashore on the very spot where Indian canoes had come to land years and years before.

The girls dragged the boat up on the beach and wrapped its rope around a nearby tree, so there would be no danger of the "April-May" drifting away if a wind blew up.

It was a very small island. A cluster of young pines and hemlocks made a grove at one end, the rest was grown over with long grasses and wild mints that lent a clean fragrance to the air. Warbling and trilling, rosy finches and dusky young juncos fluttered in and out of the tangle of birch and alders along the rocky waterline.

April thought this little island, so snug and dreaming in the sun, the most enchanting place she had ever seen. Someday she was coming back to spend an entire day lying in the wind-sweetened grass, watching the birds and the long vista of the pond between its wooded hills. And perhaps if she were lucky, she might see a deer swim the pond, as on that very first day when they had all walked down the tote road.

The pond was narrow here at the island; the deer probably swam this way when they wanted to visit the deep woods on the side opposite Deer Hill. There seemed to be an opening in the trees where the big buck had gone ashore that day. And near the beach a huge oak tree, gnarled with extreme old age, held out a sturdy, curiously bent limb that looked like a beckoning arm. April studied the oak as she ate her peanut butter sandwich and sugar cookies.

The oak looks as though it were inviting us over there to explore, she thought to herself.

"I love this little island," she said to Sally, who was eating her lunch as she sat perched on a neighboring rock. "I wish our cabin were over here."

"You come back to Maine next summer and we'll pitch a tent right here, in the shelter of the hemlocks," Sally replied promptly.

April nodded. Crescent Beach was quite forgotten in this new love for the lonely pond and the green woods.

Just as April shoved off the rowboat for the trip back, and hopped in, the two loons swam around the end of the island. April sat down quickly on the stern seat and stared eagerly at the handsome black and white birds with their proud necks ringed by white collars.

The moment they became aware of the boat drifting away from the island, the loons dove so swiftly that April wondered if she had really seen them at all. She stared at the place where they had disappeared beneath the surface. Sally, at the oars, continued to let the boat drift gently.

Minutes passed. The loons did not appear again.

"Could something have happened to them?" April wondered. "Maybe they met another big snapping turtle down there under the water."

"They'd out-swim any turtle, if they saw it first," Sally assured her. "A loon is the next thing to a fish in the water."

High, whooping laughter sounded far up the pond.

"There they are—giving us the merry ha-ha," said Sally.

April squinted her eyes for a better view across the glittering water. Finally she made out the pair of loons bobbing serenely along in single file, but then suddenly they disappeared again. After a few moments their long-beaked heads came up much closer to the boat and moved briskly down the pond. Their heads looked just like the periscopes of submarines. The effect was so odd that April burst out laughing, her clear young voice echoing over the pond. Startled, the birds shot to the surface and kept on going until it looked as if they were running on the water. Finally they took off with a strong beating of wings. They flew directly over the boat, giving April a glorious view of them, swift and shining against the sun. Then they swooped down and coasted along the pond in a shower of spray until they came to rest behind the island. Their voices rang back to the girls in clear whoops and titters.

April grinned happily at Sally, and Sally smiled back at her.

"You're getting acquainted around here," Sally said.

Back on the mainland, they tied the "April-May" to the wharf and started along the trail to the cabin. A clump of flame-colored toadstools, standing out vividly against the green of the woods, drew them off the trail for a closer look. As she stood near the toadstools, April suddenly noticed something that had been screened from the trail by a big spruce tree. She grabbed Sally's arm.

"Look!"

Sally turned. She too uttered an amazed cry.

Hidden behind the spruce was a half-faced shelter that had been skillfully woven of hemlock and spruce boughs, thatched over a framework of poles. There was no sign of any occupant. The place seemed as lonely as a deserted bird's nest.

Sally fingered a spruce tip. "The shelter was put up recently. This stuff is still green and moist."

The girls stared at each other in wordless consternation. To have imagined that they were alone in the woods and then find a man-made shelter so close to their own camp was disconcerting, to say the least. April's thoughts went to the stranger she had seen yesterday at the wharf.

"Could that strange man have built this place?" she wondered aloud. "Oh dear, I hope he isn't planning to camp here. There's no fireplace," she added, glancing about. "Surely he would have made one if he means to stay."

"I am sure Mr. Young would not give anyone else permission to camp in these woods while we are at the cabin," said Sally. "Well, the man isn't here now, so let's not worry about him."

April nodded. But it proved impossible not to think about the stranger. Both she and Sally found themselves worrying about that mysterious little shelter more than once during the rest of the day.

April awoke with a start in the still darkness next morning. Black as it was, inside and out, there was a feeling of near dawn in the air.

"Wake up, Sally!" she called across the cabin. "We don't want to miss the deer again."

A few minutes later they stole out of the cabin, two shadowy little figures in sweaters and jeans. Stars still sparkled in the sky, but the dawn breeze was ruffling the tops of the pines. The girls had to use their flashlights to find the up-hill trail, but then they switched the lights off and felt their way along as best they could. They did not want to advertise their presence to the deer until they were ready.

The going became rougher as the trail angled up hemlock-fringed ledges of granite. At the top they came out on the wood road. Sally pulled April behind some thick hemlocks.

"Let's stand quiet a while," she whispered, "and then shine our lights along the road."

As they waited, April had an eerie feeling that some living creature was near. She could not see or hear it, but she sensed it was there and the knowledge made her scalp prickle.

"I'm going to shine my light," she murmured.

The long white beam shot along the narrow road. Instantly Sally joined hers to it. April had to bite her lips to keep in a cry of delight as she saw, full in the glow of the flashlights, a beautiful doe with a little, spotted fawn standing beside her. Their ears were pricked up alertly, their big eyes were wide with wonder as they stared into the light.

The doe minced a dainty step forward, her fawn following closely.

"Ahh—" April breathed. The hand that held her flashlight trembled.

And then something big and black sprang across the road. A rough hand knocked April's flashlight to the ground, and then snatched Sally's away from her.

Both girls screamed.

"Quiet!" barked a deep voice.

The deer whisked around and disappeared up the road, their white tails high in their signal for danger.

"What are you doing here?" the voice demanded angrily of the astonished girls.

"We've got as much right to be here as you!" Sally told the tall, shadowy figure pertly. But from the way she was clutching April's arm, April knew how frightened she was.

"You girls skedaddle back to your cabin—and don't you ever leave it again after dark!" the man ordered.

Suddenly April recognized him in the dim light. He was the dark stranger she had met at the wharf! She stood as close as could be to Sally, her heart pounding heavily.

The stranger tossed Sally's flashlight back to her.

"Don't flash this light again!" He gave April a little push toward the trail. "Get going!"

Abruptly he turned and strode up the road.

Filled with a tearing urge to get away from there, the girls stumbled down the narrow trail toward the pond. They had gone but a few steps when they were brought to a shocked standstill by the sound of a rifle shot ripping the silence of the wood road behind them.

Speechless, they stood staring in the direction of the shot—the direction toward which the stranger had disappeared.

Then, far up the road, they heard the faint roar of a motor, going fast.

They did not wait for any more. Stumbling and slipping in the growing light, they legged it for their cabin as fast as they could go.

9. THE SWIMMING BUCK

THE GIRLS TUMBLED INTO the cabin and barred the door with shaking hands before they collapsed with their backs against it.

April giggled hysterically. "Anyone wanting to get at us could smash a window screen and climb in easy as pie."

Sally stood away from the door. "We're crazy. The hunter went away in his car."

"I hope so," April said bleakly. "Sally, that man who jumped at us—he's the stranger I told you about."

"And he's a jacker!" Sally's voice was grim.

April drew a deep breath like a sob. If the jacker had shot the doe, or the darling little fawn, she would have helped lure the animals to their death!

"Oh, I hope his shot missed!" she cried.

"I hope so too," said Sally. "But I'm afraid the shot found its mark. The jacker wouldn't have left so quickly if he hadn't shot a deer. He was there for business."

Sally set about making a fire. "We'll have breakfast. And then we'll go back and get your flashlight," she said firmly.

They found the flashlight where it had fallen beneath the hemlock tree.

"Let's see if we can discover where the jacker had his car hidden last night," Sally suggested.

Deer tracks were scattered thickly in the soft earth of the wood road—some were pointed toward the pond and some wove a chain back toward the top of Deer Hill. A short distance beyond where the wood road crossed the tote road, the girls came upon deep scars left by auto tires. Sally pointed to dark clots of dried blood on the bright green moss.

"The stranger got his deer," she said thinly.

April felt sick. She wanted to run away from this dark stretch of woods where only a few sunbeams could filter through the thickly interlaced branches of the pines and hemlocks.

"We ought to get word to the game warden about this shooting," Sally murmured.

131

They looked at each other unhappily.

It was a sure thing that once their folks learned that there were poachers in the woods, their days at the cabin would be numbered. Yet it seemed a base betrayal of the deer to keep what they knew from the game warden. April caught her lower lip between her teeth and moved farther away from the blood-spattered moss.

She realized now that she should have spoken to someone about the night shooting she had heard back at Deer Hill Cottage. She hadn't even told Sally about those shots.

Hesitantly she told her now. Sally listened with a troubled frown.

"So this man last night wasn't just a stray jacker," she said slowly. "The shots you heard prove that poachers have been working these woods all summer. It's a racket. Some hotels and clubs will pay high prices for out-of-season venison."

"Now that the jackers have been seen around here, perhaps they'll be afraid to come back," said April hopefully.

Sally nodded. "It could be. Let's wait before we do anything. If we hear shots tonight, we'll report them. But if everything is quiet, we won't tell the warden about the jacker until the end of the week."

Neither girl was really satisfied with this decision; they knew they should give their information to the game warden at once, even if it meant the curtailment of their stay at the cabin.

In uneasy silence they started back down the trail, glad to leave the hemlock gloom of the wood road behind them.

Back at the cabin, they changed into their bathing suits and went for a swim. As they dove off the big rock and splashed about in the clear water under the sunny blue sky, the heavy spirits caused by the discovery of jackers in their woods were gradually dispelled. The girls assured each other that the jackers would most certainly never dare return to Mik-Chik Pond, now that one of their number had been seen and could be identified. It was easy to make themselves believe this, because they so desperately wanted it to be true.

"However, we had better not do any more jacklighting on our own until we are quite positive that awful man has quit his shooting around here," Sally said, and April nodded agreement.

By noon they were ravenously hungry. They changed back into jeans and blouses, and hung their bathing suits to dry on a line stretched between two trees. Then they roasted frankfurters and heated a can of beans for lunch. Afterwards, April sprawled on her stomach in the thick shade with one of Sally's outdoor magazines spread open on the pine needles. The story of a black bear held her enthralled until the end; after finishing the story, she rolled over on her back, breathing deep of the balsam-scented air. The shy voices of pine siskins and the chirring of squirrels in the high branches overhead soon lulled her to sleep.

An hour later April sat up, brushing the pine needles out of her hair. Sally was perched on the big rock above the pool with her sketch pad and crayons. She did not even lift her head from her drawing as April got to her feet and strolled off along the trail leading to the wharf.

The afternoon hush lay deep on the forest. April walked slowly, watching the trail ahead and the woods on either side for glimpses of wildlife and flowers. She paused to pick a sprig from a clump of dark green leaves, delicately veined with white and light green. This was a new plant to her; she'd have to ask Sally about it.

She was on the wharf before she realized that a man was sitting at the end of it, looking across the pond through binoculars. She stopped in dismay. She recognized the stranger even before he turned his head.

"Hello there," he said in a friendly voice. "I was just considering borrowing your boat."

"It's not our boat," April said stiffly. "It belongs to the man who owns these woods."

"Hmm. How does it happen that you and your friend turn up in the woods at such odd hours?" the man asked. Beneath his black mustache, his lips had a humorous quirk.

He'd be awfully good-looking if he weren't such a villain, April thought irrelevantly.

Aloud, she said, "We're camping in an old cabin near here."

The stranger's eyes brightened with interest. "An old cabin," he repeated. "You mean that you two girls are camping there alone?"

April nodded.

The stranger looked at her approvingly. "You and your chum must be a couple of regular fellows."

April turned to go.

"Wait a moment," the man called, getting lightly to his feet. "Er—what's that in your hand?"

Surprised, April glanced down at the green sprig. "I don't know. Isn't it pretty!"

"Spotted wintergreen," said the stranger. "It grows thick along the old trail across the pond. Checkerberry, too."

"Old trail?" In spite of herself April was interested.

He handed her his binoculars. "Look over there. See that big oak near the pond?"

She adjusted the glasses to her eyes. The oak seemed to move close enough to touch. "It's an odd-shaped tree," she murmured. "I noticed it from the island."

"That oak was a sapling when the Pilgrims landed on Plymouth Rock. Indians bent the big branch into that unnatural position to mark the entrance to the trail over there. They often bent young trees to stand as guideposts along their wilderness trails."

April peered eagerly through the glasses.

135

"Indians coming from the north, making their summer trips to gather seafood at the mouth of the Androscoggin River, used this chain of ponds as a water road. That old oak tree marks the beginning of the portage trail across the ridge to the next pond."

April turned to give the stranger a surprised look.

"You are wondering how I happen to know all this," he said, smiling, as if he guessed her thoughts. "I have been talking to some of the old-timers around here. Local history always interests me. By the way, I want to apologize for frightening you this morning."

April stiffened. How could she have forgotten that this man was a jacker!

She thrust the glasses back into his hand and walked swiftly away. He followed her along the wharf.

"You girls shouldn't roam the woods after dark. Night time is animal prowling time. A bear or moose could give you a bad scare, if nothing worse."

April scorned to answer him. She stepped into the trail and then was brought up with a start.

She had almost bumped into Kent Oliver, who was leaning against a tree watching her and the stranger.

"Kent!" April had never been so glad to see anyone in her life.

"So long." The stranger gave April a jaunty wave of his hand as he strode past the girl and boy. He went on up the tote road and disappeared into the woods.

Kent scowled after his retreating back. "Who's that?"

136

"A man who's been hanging around here. Oh, Kent!" April burst out. "Sally and I have been so worried. We stumbled across a shelter in the woods and we think it belongs to that stranger."

"Has the fellow bothered you?" Kent demanded.

"Oh, no. But we're sure he's a deer jacker."

Kent looked startled.

"There is poaching going on. Early this morning we—we heard a shot," April finished lamely.

It flashed through her mind that if she should tell Kent that Sally and she had been roaming about in the dark, and had actually seen the jacker in action, he would surely carry the tale to Aunt Ellen and his parents, and then the camping trip would be ruined for fair.

"I heard that shot this morning," Kent said. "That is why I'm here now—to tell you you can't stay at the cabin any longer. But don't worry about the shelter. It's mine."

"Yours!"

"Yep. I've been sleeping there at night."

April stared at him speechlessly.

"It wasn't my idea," he added hastily, as he saw a storm gathering in her eyes. "Mom and your aunt were against you girls being down here alone at night, but they didn't want to spoil your fun. So I was elected to stand guard. I thought my shelter was well hidden and you'd never guess—"

"You've spoiled our camping trip!" April cried.

Her eyes flashed green and her cheeks grew pink with

anger. Kent thought she had never looked so radiantly pretty.

"Sneaking in here and snooping around when we wanted to be entirely on our own!"

"I go home right after sun-up," Kent protested. "And I've tried to keep out of your way. Even the morning you came to the cove looking for deer, you never suspected I was nearby."

April breathed a little easier. For all his spying, he did not seem to suspect that they had been in the woods at the time of the shot.

She glared at him. "Have you told your mother or Aunt Ellen about that shot this morning?"

"No. I didn't want to worry them. But I'll tell 'em fast enough unless you kids agree to come home."

"Kent Oliver! If you force us to go home I—I'll never speak to you again!"

"For Pete's sake be reasonable," he pleaded. "You just can't stay here—what with the shooting, and now this strange guy prowling about."

"I don't care! I won't have our fun spoiled any more than you've spoiled it already."

Tears of anger sparkled under April's dark lashes. She dashed them away impatiently.

"Aw, April." Kent looked miserably uncomfortable.

"You can sleep in your shelter," April conceded.

It came to her that, what with all that had been going on in these woods, it might be comforting to know that

Kent was near at night. Her voice grew a little gentler and she favored him with a glimmering smile.

"You can stay. But don't you dare tell Aunt Ellen about the poachers—or anything!"

She turned from him abruptly and ran along the trail to the cabin, not looking back.

At the cabin, April poured out the story to Sally.

"Do you think Kent will make us go home?"

Sally shrugged. "It's hard to tell about Kent. But he may decide to let us stay the week out, as long as he doesn't guess we were out in the woods when that shot was fired."

They looked at each other despairingly.

No matter whether or not they stayed at the cabin, their night adventuring in the woods was over!

After they had done the supper dishes that evening, the girls sat on the big rock in front of the cabin to watch the sunset fade and the stars wink out in the twilight. A brisk breeze kept the mosquitoes away from the shore of the pond. The scent of fern, mint, and balsam blended in a woodsy potpourri on the cool air. Far down the pond the loons were calling in high, clear voices that held a haunting note of infinite wildness and loneliness.

"They are telling us it's going to rain," said Sally.

April's eyes narrowed. Something was cutting across the starry reflections in the water.

"Sally—there's a deer swimming across the pond! Look over near the island."

139

The antlered head of a swimming deer could be dimly seen in the starlight. Breathlessly the girls watched until they lost him in the shadow of the opposite shore.

"He's going ashore at the old Indian trail."

April's words were scarcely out before a bright flash occurred near where they had last seen the deer. The report of a rifle echoed across the pond. Then the water shimmered peacefully under the twinkling stars.

For a moment the girls sat in stunned silence.

"Well!" Sally exclaimed angrily at last. "Now we know why that jacker was studying the other side of the pond through his binoculars—and fixing to use our boat."

Hand pressed to her aching throat, April stared miserably at the dark woods across the pond.

If Kent had appeared right then and ordered them to go home with him, she would have gone meekly, without a murmur of protest.

Next morning, the girls awakened to the lovely patter of raindrops on the cabin roof. April cowered under her blanket in the damp, chilly air. After a little while she hopped out of her bunk and dashed to close the blinds tight across the windows.

Outside, the pines were dripping crystal and silver, and the loons were calling lonesomely on the pond.

"This is a stay-at-home day," said April, as she hustled into her clothes.

Sally used quick-burning birch logs to build up the

fire. The small room heated in a short while, and they were able to open one of the blinds to let in light. The cold, pungent scent of the rain-washed forest came in too.

A knock sounded on the door as the girls were checking the supply shelf for rainy day breakfast ideas. They stood still a long moment in startled surprise. Finally Sally walked to the door and pulled it open. On the stone doorstep stood a stocky man in uniform. There was a bluff air of authority about him.

"Morning, girls. I'm the game warden. May I come in?"

Sally nodded permission. The warden stepped into the cabin and closed the door against the rain. His keen eyes went from one girl to the other.

"Have you seen any hunters in these woods? I've had a report that poaching and jacklighting are going on around here."

The girls exchanged apprehensive glances.

"I suppose Kent told you about the shot!" April burst out indignantly.

"No, it wasn't Kent." The warden's eyes narrowed. "What is this about a shot?"

"We've heard shots twice since coming to the cabin," Sally admitted slowly. "We saw the jacker too."

"You *saw* him! Why didn't you report it?" The warden's voice cracked like a whip. "What's he look like?"

Sally shrugged. "It was quite dark. We were stalking deer with our flashlights and—"

"Stalking deer!" The man looked flabbergasted. "Now don't tell me you girls have a gun."

"Oh, no," April cried. "We just wanted to *see* the deer."

"Now I've heard everything," said the warden with a chuckle. His face grew stern, he hooked his thumbs in his belt, and his sharp eyes seemed to bore right through the girls. "Now I want this story straight. You say you saw the jacker so you must be able to give me some sort of a description."

"He's tall and has black hair," April said hesitantly. "His skin is bronzed—and he has a little mustache."

"Hmm. And this man is the only person you've seen in the woods around here?"

Sally nodded. "We saw a buck killed last night as it was going ashore across the pond. But we didn't see who shot him."

The warden's face darkened. "Across the pond, you say! If they're going to commence operations over there, it will make it much more difficult to get them. There are no roads or good trails in that wild country. Well, thanks for the information, girls." He turned to open the door, then paused with his hand on the latch. "If you were my kids, I wouldn't have you camping down here right now."

Their faces were sober as they watched him go.

142

"Sally, will he arrest the stranger if he meets him?" April asked.

"I guess he'd have to catch him shooting deer, or with some venison actually in his possession," Sally replied.

They set about getting breakfast, in thoughtful silence. While Sally opened a can of grapefruit juice, April mixed some skillet bread of cornmeal, eggs, and dried milk and water, following a recipe for camp cooking she had found in one of Sally's outdoor magazines. She melted butter in the big iron skillet, turned in the bread mixture, put on the greased cover, and propped the skillet on its side before a bed of cherry-red coals.

From the dripping woods outside a familiar voice hailed the cabin. Sally ran to open the door.

"Hi, Kent!"

"Hi, yourself."

Kent's slicker was glistening with raindrops. Both April and Sally had a welcoming smile for him as he strode into the cabin, bringing in a gust of cold, damp air. Their feelings had changed about not wanting him around.

"You're just in time for breakfast," April greeted him.

"Mmm. Smells good." Kent took off his slicker and flung it into a corner of the room.

Sally gave him a suspicious look. "Did Mama send you down here?"

He nodded. "The game warden stopped in to see the folks after he was here. You are to come home at once."

They did not protest. Ever since the game warden's visit, they had been expecting to receive this ultimatum.

"The funny thing was that Miss Merriman was at our house even earlier than the warden," Kent continued. "She said someone stopped at the cottage to tell her it was dangerous for you girls to camp here. She seemed awfully upset about it."

"Oh, dear," sighed April.

"Were you in your shelter last night when the deer was shot across the pond?" Sally asked Kent.

He started. "What time last night? I was behind schedule with the milking and didn't reach the shelter until quite late." His hawk eyes gleamed beneath his frowning brows. "How do you know a deer was shot over there?"

"We saw it done." She told him about the swimming buck. "Someone shot it just as it was wading ashore near that big oak tree."

"It was like witnessing a murder." April's voice was choked with tears. "Oh, how I hate those jackers!"

Kent looked at her, then glanced uncomfortably away again when he saw how upset she was.

"Jacking is the lowest form of hunting," he agreed in a voice as hard and ringing as iron. "The fellow who does it hasn't a speck of sportsmanship—"

"And he's breaking the law besides," Sally said contemptuously. "On two counts: jacklighting, and shoot-

144

ing deer out of season. I hope the warden catches those poachers and claps them into jail."

Kent's mouth tightened. April had never seen his lean face set in such grim lines.

"Yeah," he snapped. "That's where jackers belong—in jail."

"The bread is done," April put in. "Let's talk about something cheerful while we have breakfast."

The skillet bread came out of the pan with a delicious golden brown crust. They served it with plenty of butter and strawberry jam. With it they had scrambled eggs and canned ham.

"You fellows sure have the knack of good camp cooking," Kent said, as they sat on the benches around the table in the glow of the fire.

The girls did their best to be gay, but the gloom of their imminent departure hung heavy over the little cabin. When the loons called across the water late that night, there would be no one at the cabin to hear them!

I'll never wake up in the night again with the fragrance of crushed hemlock clinging all about me, April thought sadly.

Kent too seemed depressed and had little to say during the meal.

"How is my earthworm business doing?" Sally remembered to ask after a while.

Kent brightened a little.

"It's keen. You've got something good there, Sis. I've

sold almost fifteen dollars' worth of worms in the short time you've been away. And I read your pamphlet." His eyes lit with enthusiasm. "Who would have thought there could be such possibilities in earthworms? Why, this thing could be built into a well-paying business!"

"I told you!" Sally reminded him. "A partnership is waiting for you any time you want it. You've been trying to think of some way to pay for a course at Forestry School—"

"That's right," Kent agreed. "Maybe earthworms are the answer."

10. THE INDIAN TRAIL

SINCE THEY HAD NO CHOICE but to leave camp, the girls made quick work of packing their clothes and left-over provisions. Kent cleaned out the fireplace, taking pains that no spark remained to cause trouble once the cabin was closed up. Everything was packed on the travois and covered with the oilcloth that had struck such a bright note on the cabin table. April did not look at Sally as they stepped outside for the last time and closed and fastened the cabin door behind them. Each knew that the other was close to tears.

Kent dragged the heavy travois up the muddy tote

road. April and Sally walked ahead of him in heavy silence, their yellow slickers and hats dripping, their cheeks cold and rosy from the rain and wind that whipped the pines on both sides of the road.

Ellen gave April an affectionate welcome back to Deer Hill Cottage.

"I *am* sorry to have spoiled your camping trip, dear," she said contritely, after Kent and Sally had helped April carry her things into the cottage and then gone on to the farmhouse. "I was so worried after that man stopped in last night to tell me the woods are unsafe because of illegal hunting."

"What man, Aunt Ellen? The game warden?"

Ellen shook her head. "He wasn't in uniform."

A startling thought suddenly came to April.

"Was he dark—with a little mustache?" she demanded.

"Why, yes. He was a handsome fellow. And he said he was a friend of yours," Ellen added with a dimpling, mischievous smile.

"Friend!" April exclaimed indignantly. "Aunt Ellen, that man is one of the deer jackers."

"Oh, no!" cried Ellen. "He—he just can't be!"

"He *is*, just the same." April wondered impatiently how her aunt could have been so completely taken in by the bold stranger. "He had a nerve coming here. He just wanted Sally and me out of the woods so there'd be no witnesses to his crimes."

Ellen still looked unconvinced, so April told her in de-

148

tail about her various encounters with the stranger. "He's a black villain," she repeated firmly. "If he comes here again, we'll just close the door in his face!"

Ellen shook her head. "I'm surprised that a man's looks could be so deceiving. And if I had dreamed that you and Sally would be foolish enough to go roaming about in the woods at night, looking for wild animals, I would never have given you permission to stay at the cabin," she added severely.

Cold rain and gusts of wind beat about the cottage all day, but bright fires in the wood-burning range and the fireplace kept the interior warm and cozy. April curled up on the couch opposite the fireplace and lost herself in the magic of *The Trail of the Sandhill Stag,* a slim book she had bought secondhand one day when she had visited the Bear Paw antique shop with her aunt. The book, with its lively drawings of deer in flight, and a frontispiece that reminded her of the magnificent buck she had seen on her first walk to the pond, had seemed just the thing for this summer's reading.

After she finished the story, she lay back on the couch, her eyes idly watching the raindrops sliding down the window panes. Sally and Kent would enjoy this book, she decided. Reading it, she had visualized Kent as Jan, the young hero. The breath of wild country and woodcraft that pervaded Ernest Thompson Seton's story seemed to belong peculiarly to Kent.

It was still raining the next morning. Looking out at

the sodden woods, April sighed as she thought of the lonely little cabin by the gray pond, its hearth cold, and no cheery curl of woodsmoke drifting above the pines from its squatty chimney. The chipmunks would miss the crumbs she had scattered for them in the mornings, but maybe the jays and the saucy red squirrels would be glad to have the clearing to themselves again.

After lunch, when she walked to the farmhouse to get some eggs for her aunt, April carried *The Sandhill Stag* buttoned inside her slicker.

A rich, chocolaty smell greeted her as she walked into the big, shabby kitchen. Sally was ironing. Kent, over by a window, was tinkering with an ancient treadle sewing machine. Chuck Young was lounging in a chair by the table, within easy reach of a plate of warm fudge.

April hung her wet slicker in the entry and crossed the kitchen to the Boston rocker, pausing on her way to help herself to a large square of fudge. She broke off a piece and gave it to Pete, who was lying near the stove with one of Tinkerbell's kittens curled up between his black paws. The kitten was purring and Pete looked as though he would like to purr too.

All the young people gave April an enthusiastic welcome, to which Pete, and Tinkerbell in the kitten basket, added their friendly acceptance of her.

"It's a good thing I came home, after all," Sally said, as she turned the shirt she was ironing. "Mama has one of her bad headaches. They always last more than one day, and if I weren't here to take over, she wouldn't have been able to go to bed and get the rest she needs."

Kent stepped over to the table for a piece of fudge. "I can't finish that thing until I get a new part," he said, nodding toward the machine.

"You'd better get one quickly then," Sally told him. "I've got a new dress cut out—I don't want to go back to school wearing jeans."

Kent scowled. "Everything in this joint is falling apart." He picked up the book April had laid on the table. "What's this?"

"A book I brought for you to read."

"The Trail of the Sandhill Stag," read Kent aloud.

"The hero reminded me of you," April said shyly.

With a piece of fudge halfway to his mouth, Chuck let out a guffaw. "Say—that's a howl," he chortled.

April blushed painfully.

Kent swung around to glare at his friend. "What's so funny?" he demanded.

"That book is a sentimental story about a fellow who tracks down a big deer and then, when his chance comes, he loses his nerve and can't shoot," Chuck said, still grinning.

"I don't see anything laughable about that," Sally said severely.

Kent stood silent, still holding the book.

"It's kid stuff, that's all." Chuck took the book and

riffled through the pages. "I remember getting all choked up over this story when I was eleven."

"I got choked up over it yesterday afternoon," April put in indignantly. "You'll love it, Kent—see if you don't," she added, looking at Sally.

"I'm sure I will. You were good to bring it to us."

April settled back in the rocker. "I didn't hear any shooting in the woods last night."

"Deer hide in dense thickets during bad weather, and don't move about much," Sally said. "So an experienced hunter wouldn't be out on a rainy night."

"Maybe. But I hope the poachers have been scared away by word that the warden is looking for them," said April.

Chuck flashed a droll glance at Kent. "Yeah, maybe the poachers lost their nerve, like the guy in this book."

Kent grabbed the book away from him. "Sometimes, feller, your sense of humor is just about nil," he snapped.

Chuck looked sulky. "Aw—what's eating you all of a sudden?"

Sally folded the last of a pile of pillow cases and switched off the iron.

"Where's that game of Scrabble Grandma sent us, Kent? I promised Chuck we'd teach him to play."

The unpleasant subject of the poachers was forgotten as the four young people gathered around the kitchen table for a lively game. April, who had been hurt by Chuck's attitude toward the book, found herself liking him again. His irresistible gaiety, and the funny words he kept spelling out on the Scrabble board, kept them all in high spirits for the rest of the afternoon.

By the time April started back to Deer Hill Cottage, the sky had cleared and a brilliant glow of color at sunset promised a fair day for the morrow. In the twilight after supper, she walked with Ellen along the road as far as the Alder place. They did not go into the yard, but just stood in the road while Ellen admired the house. April thought it looked especially spooky at dusk with the dark spruces drooping their heavy branches around it. In spite of Kent's explanation of the noises in the barn, she still had an uneasy feeling about the place. She was glad when they turned back toward Deer Hill Cottage.

"I wish I could buy an old colonial house, like the Alder place, and live in Maine always," Ellen said with a little sigh. "But it would take a mint of money to make a house like that modern and livable."

"That's right," April said absently.

She was watching the moon climb above the treetops and her fervent hope was that the good weather would not bring the jackers back again.

No sound of rifle shots disturbed her sleep that night. It really seemed as if the investigation by the warden had stopped illegal shooting in the woods of Deer Hill.

The morning dawned clear and bright. Ellen had an appointment to have her hair shampooed at a beauty parlor in Mayville, and she had some shopping to do in town. She expected to be gone almost all day. Alone in the cottage, April did her laundry and wrote a letter to her mother, without mentioning the deer poachers. That was something she would save until she was home again and her mother would not have to worry about her still being in the woods.

She stuck a stamp on her letter and sauntered down the path to Deer Hill Road. The rural mailman was just driving up in his car as she reached the mailbox. She handed him her letter and in return received one in Jean's familiar writing. April sat down at the side of the road to read it. Jean had been a faithful correspondent all summer and her letters were always lively and interesting to read. At the end of this one she had written: "Everyone has been asking me if you would surely be here for the Labor Day week end, as you promised. Tony Andrews' cousin, Bruce, is staying with him for the rest of the summer. Yesterday they invited Perry and me and June Craig to go for a sail in Tony's new boat. It's the greatest! Bruce kept saying that he wished you were along. I think he's real gone on you, April. He asked me to tell you to come in time to go to the last summer dance with him."

Thoughtfully April folded the letter. It was a warm, happy feeling to know that she was missed. And she missed her Crescent Beach friends too, ever so much, and looked forward to the Labor Day week end, when

Ellen and she expected to join the family at the beach. The dance would be fun; they always made an especially gala occasion of the last dance of the season. April had practically spent the summer in shorts and jeans, and she enjoyed the comfortable freedom of them, but it would be a delight to wear a bewitching summer dress with a froth of petticoats beneath the whirling skirt! She could apparently go to the dance with Bruce Andrews, a handsome, popular boy; that was nice also, but, strangely, not half as exciting as it would have been a year ago. April found herself wishing that it was Kent Oliver who was going to take her to the Labor Day dance.

She stood up, folded the letter, and put it into the pocket of her corduroy shorts. It was too nice a day to waste indoors. Sally was busy at home, so April decided to walk down to the pond by herself. There would be nothing to fear from the deer jackers in broad daylight.

As she crossed Deer Hill Road to the tote road, she saw Kent roll out of the farmhouse driveway in the station wagon. He tooted the horn and she waved to him. Then he turned the car in the direction of Bear Paw. April strode on, into the sun-checkered shade of the tote road.

Now that the road was so familiar, it seemed but a short walk to the wharf where the "April-May" was bobbing on her ropes. Today the pond was azure blue with a glittering chain of sun-diamonds across it. April stood on the end of the wharf looking out at the pond. It was a perfect day for a row—and there was the "April-May" practically begging her to come aboard! April frowned as she noticed the oars were tucked beneath the seats instead of being under the wharf where they belonged when not in use. It was an added proof that the jackers had used this boat to cross the pond the night they had shot the swimming buck.

But she did not want to spoil this blithesome morning by thinking about the odious jackers.

She stepped lightly into the boat and untied the ropes. A few moments later the oars were dipping and flashing rhythmically as she rowed across the pond.

Even though she missed Sally, April enjoyed being by herself on the pond. She rowed easily, resting on the oars now and then, letting the boat drift gently with the flow of the pond while she watched a hawk circle high above the top of Deer Hill. Gradually she drew closer to the other side of the pond. Turning her head, she saw the old Indian oak beckoning to her with its bent arm. She began to row steadily in that direction.

There would never be a better day to explore the Indian portage trail that led to the next lake beyond the ridge.

As she drew near shore, she swung the boat around and rowed in head-on so that she could see where she was going. Immense rocks, left by the same glacier that had scarred the top of the ridge, bulked dark in the crystal-clear depths, but the water was deep enough to float her safely to the pebbly beach near the oak. April pulled in the oars, picked up the end of the rope, and jumped ashore. A couple of turns of the rope around a sapling made the boat secure.

With a thrill April sensed the wildness of the shadowy forest that swept from the top of the ridge ahead of her down to the shore of the pond where she was standing. She gazed in awe at the burly trunk and widespread branches of the ancient oak. This tree was a living link with the past; in touching its trunk, she touched history. Two hundred years ago an Indian girl of her own age might have stood beside this oak, right where she was standing now, with her copper-colored fingers brushing the bark, just as April's fingers were touching it now. Dreamily, April wondered what the Indian girl had looked like—and to what tribe she had belonged.

As soon as she got near a library again, she was going to look up the Indian tribes of the state of Maine!

A faint trail led from the beach to the oak and on into the dim green woods. Once an Indian trail, it was now undoubtedly kept open only by the wild animals. Did bears ever come lumbering this way? April wondered. Did soft-footed wildcats prowl beneath the great oak to drink at the pond? Deer used the trail often, she knew. Her face clouded as she remembered that the swimming buck had been shot on this very beach.

Softly she stepped along the trail. There would be no one to molest either the deer or herself at this time of day. The deer were safe for now, and if she were lucky she might meet one. Not a big buck, she hoped, with a momentary return of her old-time qualms, but a dainty doe or fawn, mincing along this Indian trail that was leading her through shade so dense it was almost like walking through jewel-green water. April walked lightly, filled with a delicious, breathless feeling of high adventure.

Ahead, the trail was dappled with sunshine. April came out into a little glade, where a huge tree had crashed amid ferns, ground cedar, and pine seedlings. As she neared the fallen tree there was a slight scuffling behind it. Her breath caught in her throat. She stopped short, tense and wary, in spite of her former desire to meet some wildlife.

Again came a sound of flurried movement, and with it a tiny bleat, scarcely more than a sigh, as of pain. The pathetic sound sent April slowly forward. She reached the tree and glanced timidly over it. A cry of wonder burst from her as a small animal struggled up from the ground, tottered a few steps away from her, and then fell down.

It was a spring fawn, its reddish coat spangled with silver spots. One of its front legs was injured, yet it might have been able to hop away on three legs if it had not been weakened by bleeding. The ferns, where it had been lying when April surprised it, were stained by dark clots of dried blood.

"You poor little thing!" April cried.

The fawn seemed more frightened by the sound of her voice than he had been at the human smell of her. Once more he tried to get away, only to sprawl helplessly on the moss. His big eyes stared at April with a trapped look that wrung her heart.

She twisted her hands in helpless pity. She longed to do something to aid the young, suffering creature, but did not know at all how to go about it. She could see a deep, bloody gash on the upper part of one of the fawn's slender front legs. How had he been hurt? Where was his mother?

After a moment of anxious indecision, April scrambled over the log, murmuring tender words that she meant to be reassuring to the trembling fawn. Then she looked anxiously about the little glade, wondering if perhaps the mother were hiding somewhere near.

Suddenly there stole over April an uneasy feeling of being watched by hostile eyes. At the same moment the fawn's sensitive nostrils flared as if a whiff of terrifying scent had come to them. His ears twitched nervously. He seemed to forget April as his wide eyes searched the edge of the forest, seeking the source of the scent that had frightened him.

Following the fawn's wide gaze, April turned and her eyes probed the gently stirring shadows. The trees and bushes seemed to melt together to form an impenetrable green wall around the glade. Anything could be hiding there, and April was sure that something was. Something sinister and frightening.

Her eyes kept going back to the dense green branches of a large hemlock growing at the edge of the forest. Something about that tree gave her a prickly sensation at the roots of her hair. She fancied she could see the glitter of pale, savage eyes through the screen of green needles. She went cold with terror. She started to run away, but then she remembered the fawn and went back to take her stand beside it. Choked with terror, she glared desperately at the hemlock. She was sure that whatever was hidden in its branches was getting ready to spring, either at the fawn or at herself.

"Scat!" She tried to scream at the thing, but her voice came out in a croak.

April reached down and grabbed the fawn from behind, locking her hands around him. He did not struggle; he seemed to be stunned by the touch of human hands. To April it was like picking up a frozen thing. The fawn wasn't any heavier than a medium-sized dog, but his long, slender legs got in the way and made him awkward to handle. Crushing him against her, she ran clumsily back along the trail to the pond. All the way she was stiff with fear lest the bear, or wildcat, or whatever had been hiding in that hemlock, jump on her back.

Panting and stumbling, she lugged the fawn down to the ancient oak and dumped him into the rowboat. She pulled the ropes free and pushed the boat into deep water; then she made a flying leap, tumbled into the boat, and sank down breathlessly on the rower's seat.

Not until she was a couple of oar lengths from shore did April breathe easily again. Wide-eyed still from her frightening experience, she looked back at the dense green woods as her steady rowing took her further and further away from them. There was no sign of life along the Indian trail or among the trees, but she knew she had not just been imagining danger back there in the glade. Some animal had been hiding in that hemlock! The threat to the fawn—and probably to herself as well—had been real.

She glanced over her shoulder to see where the boat was headed, and there was the island, dead ahead, as if in answer to the question of what to do with the wounded fawn.

Of course! The island was the very place for him. It had trees for shelter; bushes, grass, and herbs for food. No other animals were there, and human hunters would never suspect the presence of a deer on such a little patch of ground. With quick strokes she pulled for the beach where she and Sally had landed a few days ago.

The fawn lay in a heap in the bottom of the boat, watching her with soft eyes that were filled with fear and wonder. His velvet sides heaved with deep-drawn breaths, but other than that he lay as still as a sunbeam.

April saw with concern that his wound was bleeding again.

Suddenly she noticed other, older dark stains on the bottom of the boat.

Some other animal, wounded or dead, had crossed the pond in this boat, and not long ago. It might have been the fawn's mother, for surely she never would have deserted the injured fawn if she were alive.

For the first time April realized that the fawn's wound had probably been caused by a bullet. The jackers had been at work again on that side of the pond!

Shuddering, she pictured to herself what might have happened the night before: poachers hunting on the Indian trail—the doe and her fawn attracted by the lure of the powerful jacklight. Then two rifle shots in quick succession—the doe killed, but the fawn, who had been a few steps behind her, only wounded. Wild with pain and terror, the little fellow must have hobbled away on three legs to hide in some dense thicket. The jackers would not have dared linger long to search for him, because there was a possibility that the game warden had heard their shots and might be hot on their trail. The thought of leaving a wounded fawn to die a lingering death would not have troubled them in the least.

April's lips trembled as she thought of what the fawn must have suffered in bewilderment and terror during the long, dark hours of loneliness and pain. She longed to comfort him and pet him, but she was afraid her touch would panic him and that he might try to jump out of the boat. She contented herself with a glance of sympathy and pity.

"You are safe now," she whispered brokenly, "I'm going to take care of you."

11. FIRST AID FOR A FAWN

THE BOAT GRATED ON the island beach, and April jumped ashore and tied up. When she turned to help the fawn, she found him trying to struggle out of the boat by himself. She reached for him, but he shrank away from her and uttered a shrill, heart-wrenching cry for his vanished mother.

Tears came to April's eyes. "Please let me help you," she begged.

Somehow she managed to get hold of him and drag him ashore. He hopped away on his three good legs and collapsed in the long, sweet grass. Breathless from the exertion of trying to handle him, April glanced around at the sun-drenched little island, quiet except for the twitter of birds in the thickets.

"Nothing will harm you here," she assured the fawn. "And I'll be back very soon.".

It was hard to leave him, for there was no way of letting the poor thing know that he wasn't being deserted again.

She ran to the boat, shoved it into deep water as she scrambled in over the bow, and pulled for the mainland with quick, easy strokes that sent the tubby craft skipping over the water. As she neared the shore she saw Kent walk out on the wharf.

"Hi!" he called across the water.

April pulled in her oars and Kent caught the bow of the boat as it nosed alongside the wharf. He made the boat fast, and then gave April his hand to help her up on the wharf.

"I saw you heading for the tote road this morning, when I was starting for Bear Paw to get Ma's medicine," he said. "I thought you might like company for the walk home."

"Oh, Kent, I've had such a time!" she cried. "There's a wounded fawn on the island—"

"Are you kidding?"

"No, no. I found it over on the old Indian trail, near where the other deer was shot."

The story came tumbling out. As Kent listened, his thin, tanned face took on a grim expression.

"So they're killing fawns now," he muttered.

"And using our boat to cross the pond," April said indignantly. "There are blood stains in the boat, and not just from my fawn."

She glanced anxiously across the water at the island. Was the fawn still bleeding?

"Will you row over to the island with me, Kent? The fawn needs help."

"I don't see what more we can do. You've taken the critter to a place where it will be comparatively safe."

"The wound must be treated," April explained. "Please help me, Kent. I can't handle the poor thing by myself without hurting it."

The pleading look in her hazel-green eyes was irresistible to Kent. "Okay," he said gruffly, "let's go."

"Wait here until I get some things from home."

She raced up the tote road as fast as she could go.

At the cottage, April, still breathless from her climb, rummaged distractedly in the refrigerator and the kitchen cupboard. What did a fawn eat besides grass and such? Finally she took a quart of milk from the refrigerator, then added half a coffee cake in case the fawn had a sweet tooth. The cottage did not offer much in the way of medical supplies; April discarded the idea of using iodine, because she wasn't sure whether an animal's reaction to it would be beneficial. She decided that if she could cleanse the wound and bind it up to prevent further bleeding, nature would do the rest. Into her basket with the milk and coffee cake went a package of pure white soapflakes, a white enamel pan for heating water, a bowl for the milk, and a clean pillowcase to tear up for bandages.

Munching a molasses cookie, because she hadn't had any lunch, April tore back down the road to the pond.

During her absence, Kent had busied himself scouring away the tragic dark spots in the boat. When he saw April run out on the wharf, he washed his hands, took her basket, and helped her aboard. She sat facing Kent as he rowed, the breeze tumbling her brown hair about her cheeks and the sun threading it with ruddy gold. She smiled brightly at Kent, happy to have his company on this adventure.

"Could it really have been a wildcat that frightened us so, over on the trail?" she asked.

"There are bobcats around here," Kent admitted. "Although a fellow hardly ever sees one. They follow the deer, and there are more deer on that side of the pond than over here."

"Then, if I hadn't happened along, the bobcat would have killed the fawn," April said with a shiver. "Maybe it was getting ready to attack me, too. I had the strangest feeling that something awful would happen if I didn't get out of there quick."

"A wildcat wouldn't go for you unless it was starving,

and summer isn't starving time in the woods." Kent rowed a while in thoughtful silence. "Still it's just as well that you didn't linger in that glade, because there's always some animal that does not follow the general pattern of behavior for its kind. Nine cats might let you go, or run away from you. The tenth might jump you."

The oars dipped and flashed to his steady rowing. A playful breeze was ruffling the surface of the pond and the water slapped and chuckled against the bow of the "April-May."

"The woods are so beautiful," said April. "Why do they have to be spoiled by ferocious killers like wildcats!"

"The cats only kill to live and feed their young, same as other animals," Kent reminded her. "And it would be far better for a bobcat to kill your fawn clean than for the little guy to die a lingering death of his wound."

"Oh, no!" April protested in horror.

"No sense in not being realistic. The real villains are the men who shot the fawn and left it to die," Kent said angrily.

"I—I suppose that's true," April admitted.

"Sure is," Kent said in a gentler tone. "Some animals are meat eaters because that is nature's way of keeping a proper balance of life in the forest. If cats and bears didn't take toll of the deer herd, the deer would multiply so that they would soon overgraze the woods and starve to death. They would make themselves more of a nuisance to farmers, for they would do even greater raiding of fields and young orchards than they do now. All these things have happened in protected areas where neither the deer's natural enemies nor men have hunted them."

April was listening attentively, her hands folded in her lap.

"I guess every creature on earth was put here for some good purpose," Kent mused.

April's eyes began to dance. "Then even that old snapping turtle, who ate ducklings and fish, must have been part of nature's plan. And you were messing things up when you took him away to be made into soup," she added severely.

A slow grin lighted Kent's strong-featured face.

"I guess you've got me there, April. Yes, the same rule holds for fish as for other wild creatures. In the old days, before white settlers came to New England, mink, otter, turtles, eagles, and ospreys helped the Indians keep the fish population from choking the ponds and streams. Now our civilization has brought pollution to many streams, so we don't need the eagles and mink to keep the fish under control. We poison the streams and kill 'em off that way," he said ruefully.

April looked at him with sincere admiration.

"You know an awful lot about the woods, Kent."

"I've been a woods runner ever since I learned to walk," he said slowly. "Pop taught me to fish and shoot when I was only knee-high. But, even more than hunting, I've always liked to study wild creatures. There is something about the woods that can really hold a fellow."

He paused abruptly, looking embarrassed, even shy.

April realized with a glow of happiness that Kent probably did not talk like this about himself to many people.

"You talk something like Jan—you know, the boy who hunted the Sandhill Stag. Did you read that book, Kent?"

"Yep. It's a good story."

"I was so glad that Jan finally let the stag go. Oh!" April cried passionately, "how can men shoot a beautiful creature like a deer and call it sport!"

Kent's face clouded.

"And the jackers! Oh, what brutal, heartless people they must be."

"Yeah, they're a bad lot," Kent agreed heavily.

He beached the boat on the island and tied it up. April ran eagerly through the long grass to where she had left the little deer. A cry of dismay flew back to Kent.

"The fawn is gone!"

Kent came up with the basket. "He couldn't go far if he's as bad hurt as you say. He's probably hiding in those hemlocks."

They walked toward the hemlocks, going slowly so as not to frighten the fawn. Kent put the basket down on the ground and stole into the hemlock grove. A moment later April heard a plaintive bleat, and then the fawn came hopping in startled haste from the shelter of the trees.

April dropped to her knees. "Come here," she murmured, holding out her hand, "I want to help you."

Standing on three legs, the fawn gave her a wide, questioning glance; then it hopped a step closer and lay down in the grass. Its silver-dappled, red-brown coat shimmered richly in the sun.

"You darling, lovely thing," April whispered.

Inch by inch she crawled closer to the quiet fawn. She guessed that the little deer was too weak from loss of blood to jump up and run away from her. Also, they had been through a lot together, and perhaps he was beginning to trust her a little.

At last she was close enough to put out her hand and gently stroke the fawn's sleek head. He quivered at her touch, but did not try to get away. He was lying so that his weight would not rest on the torn front leg, where blood was seeping in slow drops from the ugly lips of the bullet wound. April felt as though her heart would burst with love and pity.

Kent was watching from the edge of the hemlocks. He started to walk toward them, but stood still when the fawn's head jerked up in alarm.

"I've hunted some," he burst out. "But I've never shot at a fawn, or left a wounded animal to die in the woods."

He appeared to be almost as wrought up about the fawn as April herself.

April stood up, trying to keep all her movements gentle and unalarming.

"Please bring me the basket, Kent."

After he fetched it, she poured half the bottle of milk into the bowl and set it down before the fawn. The fawn's delicate nostrils dilated. He struggled to his feet and began to lap the milk eagerly. After he had drunk almost all there was in the bowl, he lay down again to rest. But soon he was up and at the milk again.

April crumbled the coffee cake and strewed bits of it near the fawn, but, for the present at least, all that interested him was the milk.

Kent squatted down for a closer look at the fawn's hurt leg.

"It's a deep gash," he said at last. "The bullet probably grazed the bone. But from the way he holds that leg, I don't think the bone is broken. If he would lick the wound, it might heal by itself. The bullet isn't there; I can see where it came out at the back."

"I think we should cleanse the wound and tie it up so that flies can't get at it," April insisted.

They made a fire of twigs and driftwood on the beach. Kent filled the pan with water and set it on two stones to heat. April tore the pillowcase into strips, and mixed a mild solution of soap and boiled water. When everything was ready, she gave Kent a pleading look. "Will you wash the wound?"

He nodded grimly. "I thought I'd get that job."

April held the fawn firmly between her knees while Kent cleansed the bullet wound with soap and water. April kept whispering to the fawn to be brave, but he trembled and shrank against her. Kent gritted his teeth as he worked on the wound. Once he looked up and his troubled eyes met April's.

"I'll never again take pride in shooting," he muttered.

April nodded. Her lips were trembling.

Working swiftly, even if awkwardly because of the fawn's frightened struggles, Kent bound the lengths of white cloth around the wounded leg. "If the critter doesn't get blood poisoning, he'll be okay in a few days," he said, as he finished the bandaging and stood up.

April let the fawn go. "At least we've stopped the bleeding."

The fawn hobbled over to the hemlocks and lay down in the shade. April poured the rest of the milk into a bowl and placed it near him.

"We've done all we can," said Kent. "It's time I got home to do my chores."

"I'll bring your breakfast tomorrow," April told the fawn.

The girl and boy walked away toward the boat. The fawn struggled to his feet and tried to hobble after them, but his bandaged leg was too stiff and sore for him to go

173

far. Poised on three legs, his delicate head high, his soft eyes mutely pleading, he stood in the grass and watched them row away.

Kent did not talk at all on the way back to the wharf. After tying up the boat, he strode up the tote road at a pace that had April trotting breathlessly to keep up.

"Goodness," she panted, "what's the hurry?"

"I've got a job to do that has needed doing a long, long time," he said tersely.

When they reached Deer Hill Road, April saw that her aunt's car was still gone from its parking space. She just had to tell someone about the day's adventures, so she walked on to the farmhouse with Kent. In the driveway he turned to her suddenly.

"I want to tell you one thing," he said in a hard voice, "if I can help it, there'll be no more shooting of deer in these woods."

"Oh, if only you *could* do something, Kent!"

"I can and will! When they begin slaughtering fawns, it's time someone put a stop to it."

He strode on to the barn. Even the set of his broad shoulders looked angry.

April gazed after him for a moment and then walked to the house to look for Sally.

12. THE JACKERS

SALLY WAS SITTING on the kitchen doorstone shelling peas, while Pete kept her company in the grass nearby. The kittens were all asleep in a heap in the woodshed, and Tinkerbell had strolled off to inspect the mouse runs in the barn. April sank down on the stone slab beside Sally.

"Oh Sally, I have so much to tell you! I rowed across the pond this morning, to explore the old Indian trail—"

Sally snapped a pea pod and spilled the tender green peas into a bowl in her lap. "You wouldn't have dared venture into those woods by yourself a few weeks ago," she reminded April with a laugh.

April laughed too. "That's right. What a scairdy cat I was! But I was plenty frightened today, let me tell you."

She poured out the story of her rescue of the fawn.

Sally stopped shelling peas to listen. She was both enthralled and horrified.

"So the jackers are still at their wicked work!" she cried, when April had finished her story. "How long is it going to keep on?"

April had never seen Sally so upset.

"The game warden has a lot of territory to cover," she reminded her. "He'll probably be arresting the jackers any day now."

Somehow this thought did not seem to make Sally any happier.

"Isn't it strange," April continued, "that we always speak of the jackers in the plural, although we have actually seen only one man. Somehow I've always had the feeling that there are several of them at work here."

Sally put down the dish of peas and got to her feet. "Let's walk down the road a way."

Pete lifted his head to watch wistfully as the girls walked down the path to the road. Finally he got up, and after a quick look to make sure that his cat friends were still safe in the woodshed, he trotted after Sally.

Sally's usually bright face was clouded and unhappy.

"I want to tell you something I couldn't talk about at the house for fear Mama would hear."

"What's troubling you?" April asked anxiously.

"It's Kent," Sally said in a low voice. "He's been acting so strangely of late. Last night I came on him in the barn. He was cleaning his gun and he was just furious to have me catch him at it. He said he had been shooting at a hawk, but I haven't noticed any hawks bothering our chickens. April—" Sally stared ahead miserably. "I wouldn't tell anyone but you. I'm scared that Kent is mixed up with the jackers."

A chill stole through April's veins. "That's a terrible thing to say about your brother."

"I don't want to think so. But Kent is surely up to something."

They walked a way in heavy silence.

"Remember the day we found Tinkerbell's kittens?" Sally murmured. "You thought you saw something hanging in the Alder barn. Well, I've been wondering if you mightn't have seen a deer. That barn would be a good place to hang venison. Mr. Young seldom goes out to inspect the place, as Kent well knows."

April thought back to that day. "But when we went back into the barn the thing was gone."

"Kent was in the barn. Remember? He could have pulled the deer down to fool us in case we went back in, which we did. Then he scared us away with those eerie owl noises."

"We never would have known Kent was there that day, if George Crawly hadn't come with his truck and got tough with you."

The truck!

Both girls gasped and swung to face each other as though the same unpleasant thought had occurred to each of them.

"That truck came to pick up the venison!" April cried.

"George Crawly and Kent must be in this together," Sally said shamefacedly. "And the truck driver was a dark man with a mustache. We didn't get a very good look at him—"

April nodded. "It must have been the stranger. The first time I met him at the wharf, I thought that I had seen him somewhere before."

A tight knot seemed to be tied in her heart. To think that Kent might be in league with those others to jack-light deer!

They turned into the Alder driveway and walked straight to the barn.

"If they killed your fawn's mother last night, the venison may still be here, waiting for the truck to come and pick it up," said Sally. "If we find it, we'll notify the game warden at once."

"The warden may arrest Kent," April protested.

That thought made Sally hesitate a moment. She stared unhappily at the closed barn door, then she drew a deep breath and pushed it open. With a sinking heart April followed her inside.

Their eyes, accustomed to the bright daylight outside, could make out only dimly the objects that were hanging from the barn rafters. They went closer and saw two deer, dressed out neatly like beef for the market and swathed in cheesecloth to protect the meat from flies.

April thought of the fawn, wounded and left alone to die in the forest. One of these deer was probably its mother. She smothered a sob.

Oh, if Kent had done this thing!

The girls could not get out of the barn quickly enough. "What can we do?" Sally appealed to April. "Whoever is shooting the deer should be reported. But it will kill my mother if it *is* Kent and he gets arrested."

She started to cry. April put her arm around her, and Pete nosed her hand, as if he sensed her unhappiness and wanted to comfort her too.

While they were standing there in wretched indecision about what to do next, a truck turned into the driveway and screeched to a stop a few feet away from them. George Crawly got out. With him was the dark driver, and April noted with a queer feeling of relief that the man was *not* the stranger.

The driver went into the barn. George stopped to give the girls an ugly scowl.

"What are you two nosing about here for this time?"

Sally flung up her head proudly. "We're going to tell the game warden about those deer in the barn."

George's jaw dropped, but then he recovered his nerve and stepped toward her threateningly.

"You're crazy! You'd better keep your mouth shut about what goes on around here!"

The truck driver came out of the barn with the carcass of a deer balanced on his shoulder. He slung it into the truck and went back inside the barn. April watched in agitated silence.

"You squeal to the warden and your brother will go to jail," George told Sally in a threatening voice.

Pete was standing beside Sally with his gleaming eyes fixed on George's face. The setter's mouth was set in a wolfish snarl. He growled deep and low.

"Kent shot those deer," George went on, "we're just picking them up."

"Then Kent will have to take his medicine along with you," Sally said thinly.

She started to walk away.

"Wait!" George yelled. He grabbed her arm so roughly that she cried out in pain. "Now you listen to me," he growled and swung her about to face him again.

"Let go of her!" April cried angrily.

"You stay out of this!" George shouted.

With a tearing growl, Pete sprang at George and bowled him over backwards. George let out a frightened yell. April screamed as she saw the youth writhing on the ground, struggling to hold the raging dog away from his throat. Sally tried to call Pete off, but her voice was lost in the clamor of George's frenzied cries and the snarling and worrying of the infuriated dog.

Suddenly another voice rang above the commotion.

"Pete! Here, boy! *Pete!*"

Kent had come pelting down the driveway from the road. He grabbed Pete's collar and dragged him away from George. Pete kept right on snarling and he strained to get back at George, who lay with his arm across his face, too badly scared to get up.

The truck driver came rushing out of the barn. He glowered at the group in the driveway, but made no attempt to go to the assistance of his partner.

"What's up?" he demanded roughly.

George got slowly to his feet. He was clutching his left arm, and blood dripped between his fingers from the scratches made by Pete's teeth. He glared at the dog.

"You're a dead dog the first time I get out here with my gun," he rasped.

"You won't be coming out to Deer Hill again with your gun, George," Kent said grimly, still clinging to Pete's collar.

"Who says?" George snarled. "You want to keep the racket to yourself now it's paying off?"

Sally's hand met April's and clung tightly.

Kent turned to the girls. "You two go home!" he ordered.

They stared at him, heartsick.

George laughed mockingly. "They know you're a jacker, Kent. I told them you shot those two deer last night."

"That's a lie—and you know it's a lie!" Kent blazed. "I haven't shot a deer since the girls went to camp at the cabin. And I've never done any night hunting, or even knew that you fellows were using jacklights around here until I heard shooting in the woods a few nights ago— after you had promised me you'd stay out of the woods around Mik-Chik Pond while the girls were at the cabin."

"You were nuts if you expected me to keep that promise," George sneered.

Kent gave the girls a pleading look, as though he were begging for their understanding and charity.

"I did my hunting in the mornings on the hill—"

"Then it's true, you *are* a poacher," Sally said brokenly. "The day we found Tinker's kittens you were in the barn, and April saw deer hanging in there—"

"Your fine brother shot those deer that very morning, and he was waiting in the barn for us to come and pick them up and pay him for 'em," George sneered.

"I ought to punch your head, Crawly!" Kent said furiously.

"Yeah? And what would that prove?"

April felt numb and cold. She was as stunned as if someone had told her that Perry had robbed a bank.

Kent Oliver a deer poacher! Oh, it simply could not be true!

Kent was still holding Pete. "Yes, I shot the two bucks that were hanging in the barn that day," he confessed through tight lips. "But now I've quit hunting. And so have you fellows, at least around here."

George's partner carried the second deer out of the barn and heaved it into the truck.

"Who's gonna quit when we're all making money?" he boomed, jerking a tarpaulin over the venison.

He walked around the truck and got in behind the wheel.

"Come on, Crawly. We got other stops to make."

George scrambled up beside him.

Kent let go his hold on Pete's collar and stepped close to the truck.

"I went into this rotten business because I needed money," he said grimly. "I wasn't proud of myself from the first, but now that it's come to jacking and slaughtering fawns, I've had enough. I quit. And I'm going to see to it that all poaching stops on Deer Hill."

"Fawn meat comes high," George replied in his rasping voice. "We didn't ask you to shoot fawns, Sir Galahad, but what we do, and where we do it, is our own business. We'll shoot where we please. And if you know what's good for you, you'll string along with us."

"Let's get going—we got meat to deliver," the other man reminded George impatiently.

He started the motor and began to back the truck around.

"Remember what I said," Kent shouted. "You're through. If there is any more shooting around Mik-Chik Pond, I'll go to the warden."

"You won't have to go to him, Kent. He's right here," said a quiet voice from the other side of the truck.

George turned to look at two men who had suddenly left their place of concealment in the woodshed. His jaw dropped. His partner stalled the truck. April, Sally, and Kent stood transfixed in stunned surprise.

One of the men was the game warden, the other was the tall dark stranger who had been haunting the woods of Deer Hill.

"Make a run for it!" George urged the truck driver hoarsely.

The game warden whipped out his revolver and pointed it at the truck. "Stay right where you are!"

The stranger sprang to the back of the truck and jerked aside the tarpaulin that covered the venison. "Here's our evidence," he called to the warden.

Kent pulled April and Sally back against the barn. "There could be a fight. You shouldn't be here," he told them.

The stranger looked around at them. "That's right. You girls run along home!"

"You go, April," Sally murmured. "I want to stay with Kent."

April stood her ground. Sally needed her.

"You can come along to the Judge right now," the warden told George and his partner. He turned to the stranger and said, "You drive this truck to the village."

He made the two poachers get out of the truck and slipped handcuffs on them.

"You want Kent Oliver too," George spat out. "He's one of the ring."

Sally gave a low sob. April slipped her arm through Sally's.

Kent stared straight ahead, avoiding the warden's searching eyes.

"And Chuck Young is another who is in on this," George informed the warden.

At that Kent swung around indignantly. "Chuck shot only one deer!" he burst out.

"One deer is one too many out of season, Kent," the warden said seriously. "You and Chuck know that."

"Yes sir, I know," Kent muttered miserably.

"You'll have to appear before the Judge with these men," the warden said. "I'd like your father to come with you. I'll get Chuck and Mr. Young."

"You can drive to the village with me, Kent," the stranger offered.

Kent's shoulders drooped. "Thanks. But Pop and I will go in by ourselves, if that's okay with the warden."

"Very well," agreed the warden. "I'll expect you and your father to meet me at Judge Garfield's office in an hour." He sighed and shook his head. "I would have bet my last nickel, Kent, that you were as square as they come."

The warden strode heavily out of the yard and across the road to where his car was hidden in a nearby farm lane. He drove into Deer Hill Road, and the stranger herded George Crawly and his handcuffed partner out to the car and made them get in. Then he climbed into the cab of George's truck and followed the warden's car toward Bear Paw.

Kent hadn't looked at either his sister or April since the warden had told him he must appear before Judge Garfield. Now, without a word, he strode out of the yard and down the road toward home. April and Sally followed in painful silence, and Pete trotted soberly at their heels, as if he realized that his family was in trouble.

April watched Kent's tall figure disappear around a curve in the road ahead.

He probably wishes he could find a fox den somewhere and crawl inside to stay for keeps, April thought bitterly.

Her heart ached for Sally, whose bright bounciness had all disappeared. Sally kept a tight hold on April's hand. Every so often she gave a broken sob. April longed to comfort her, but what was there to say?

They stopped in the road by the Oliver driveway.

"I hate to go in," Sally confessed. "My mother and father are going to take this very hard."

Her troubled brown eyes sought April's. "Do you think the Judge will send Kent to jail?"

April stared at her. The thought of Kent Oliver in jail was staggering. Yet, of course, that was where they sent people who committed crimes.

"I—I don't know," she said uncomfortably.

Sally's capable hand tugged nervously at a button on her blouse. "Now I know how Kent expected to earn money for the tractor. But how *could* he!" she blazed. "A deer poacher! Doesn't he realize we'd rather lose the farm altogether than have him do anything like that?"

"He was thinking only of helping the family through hard times," April said gently.

She said the words to comfort Sally, but deep down in her own aching heart they made a single warm spark in the new coldness of her feeling toward Kent.

13. APRIL AND KENT

ELLEN WAS AT THE KITCHEN counter preparing supper when April burst into the cottage. She looked around at her niece with a smile.

"How do you like my hair?"

April had no thought for anything but her own grim news.

"Aunt Ellen! Kent Oliver is the deer poacher!"

Ellen almost upset the bowl of salad she was mixing. She put down the wooden spoon and fork and stared blankly at April.

"Where did you hear that ridiculous bit of news?"

"I was there when the game warden arrested him."

"It can't be!" Ellen said numbly. "A nice boy like Kent."

"I thought he was nice too."

April ran to her room and threw herself down on the bed. In spite of her brave attempt to comfort Sally and herself with the assurance that Kent's motives had been unselfish, the hard, cold fact remained that he had been slaughtering the wild deer. Kent, whom she thought loved the deer and all wild creatures as much as she herself had learned to love them during this summer in Maine.

Ellen came into the room and sat down on the bed beside her.

"Tell me how you learned about Kent," she said, gently smoothing April's tumbled hair.

In a muffled voice April described the doings at the Alder place.

"Sally had begun to fear that Kent might be involved with the jackers. But, until he admitted it himself, I just wouldn't believe that he could be so cruel and dishonest."

She wiped her eyes on her sleeve and sat up, her face red and puffy from crying.

"It seems the game warden knew there were deer in the Alder barn today, and he was hiding in the woodshed, waiting for the truck to come so he could arrest the jackers with the venison in their possession. Sally and I just happened to arrive there at about the same time as the truck. Then Kent showed up, too. I guess he came on purpose to tell George Crawly that he was through with poaching, and that George couldn't hunt on Deer Hill any more. Kent was awfully mad because he had discovered that the jackers have been killing fawns," she added, almost grudgingly. "So there we were: the jackers, Kent, Sally and I, the game warden, even Pete, all milling about in the Alder driveway. And you know that man with the little black mustache, the one I thought was a jacker? He must be another warden, because he was hiding in the woodshed too."

Ellen laughed softly. "I have a confession to make, dear. I have been keeping a secret from you, but only because Mr. Alder asked me not to reveal his identity until he had stopped the poaching in his woods. He hoped the jackers would take him for a tramp if they caught him prowling about."

"Mr. Alder!" April exclaimed in consternation.

Ellen nodded. "Your mysterious stranger is Jim Alder, our favorite author. He introduced himself to me when he came here to warn me that it wasn't safe for you girls to stay at the cabin. He had come back to his birthplace without telling anyone, and he put up at the Bear Paw Inn with the intention of living there until his own house could be made ready for occupancy. Not even the Youngs knew he was back. The very first morning after he arrived at Bear Paw, he came out to Mik-Chik Pond to fish at dawn and he heard shots in the woods."

Probably the same shots I heard one morning, April thought to herself.

"Mr. Alder suspected poachers, of course, but he did not see them," Ellen continued. "Later that day, prowling about his place, he discovered signs that made him suspect the jackers were using his barn as a place to hide their illegally killed venison. He informed the game warden, and they set themselves to catch the poachers."

"That's why I was always meeting him in the woods," April murmured. "And was I ever stupid! I should have guessed who he was the day he told me about the old Indian trail."

Ellen stood up. "Bathe your face now, April. After supper we'll walk over to the Olivers. It's good for people to be reminded that they have friends when trouble comes."

Later, before they could get started for the Olivers, a knock sounded on the cottage door. Thinking it might be Sally, April flew to open the door. But it was Jim Alder who was standing on the doorstep, handsome and distinguished looking in tailored tweeds.

How could I have been so dumb as to think he was a jacker? April wondered in acute embarrassment.

Her cheeks burned under his smiling glance.

"Good evening, April," he said in his warm, vibrant voice.

April wished she could sink through the floor. Ellen hurried to her rescue.

"How nice to see you, Mr. Alder," she said graciously. "Won't you come in?"

She invited him to take one of the easy chairs before the fireplace. The night was cool and the bright fire of birch and apple logs made the room cozy and inviting.

"Nice place Oliver has here," Jim Alder said appreciatively.

He handed April a large pink and gold box of chocolates.

"An apology for not having introduced myself properly the first time we met."

His friendly manner made her feel less flustered.

"I'm the one who should apologize," she said, liking him more and more. "The way we made free with your cabin and all."

Jim and Ellen took opposite chairs by the fire, and April sat on the couch.

"I couldn't think of a nicer thing to happen to that old cabin than to have you and Sally camping there," Jim assured April. "I used to camp there every summer when I was a boy."

"April has been telling me how the poachers were arrested," Ellen said.

Jim nodded and April saw that he was admiring the

rich play of the firelight in the silky blondness of Ellen's hair.

April leaned forward to ask the question that was burning on her lips.

"Did—did the Judge send Kent Oliver to jail?"

"No," said Jim. "Kent and my young cousin, Chuck, both admitted to shooting deer out of season, but they denied ever having done any jacklighting, and the Judge and game warden were inclined to believe them. Kent seems to be too much of a genuine sportsman at heart to have engaged in such a nefarious practice. Chuck too, I hope. But Chuck was more at fault than Kent in this matter of poaching; his excuse was simply that he wanted some excitement, while Kent went into it with the mistaken idea of earning money to help his family through hard times."

"He's always worrying about how hard his father has to work and how they need just everything for the farm," April said in a low voice.

"Mr. Oliver is not a well man," Ellen explained. "Kent shoulders a lot of his father's responsibilities."

"So I understand," said Jim. "But Kent has not helped his father by breaking the law. Mr. Oliver was pretty well broken up when he learned what Kent had been up to."

"It's hard to believe that a boy like Kent could become involved in a sordid business like poaching," Ellen sighed.

Jim nodded. "We discovered today that George Crawly's friend is the head of a poaching ring that extends over a large territory. George, being a local boy, knows that deer are plentiful around Mik-Chik Pond and that Kent is a good shot. They got at Kent just at the time when he was particularly worried about his family's financial problems. He shot a few deer for them, but soon became disgusted with the furtive hunts, the hiding of the venison, and all the other unpleasant facets of poaching. Before today he had warned George that he would do no more illegal hunting. But of course he must still take his punishment."

"You said he didn't have to go to jail," April reminded Jim.

She wondered why she should still care what happened to Kent.

"That's right," Jim told her. "Kent and Chuck have been boys of good character and behavior until this incident. If they ever repeat their crime, it will go very hard with them, but this time the Judge let them off with a stiff lecture and a fine of one hundred dollars and costs each, the money to be earned by the boys themselves. Whether or not their hunting licenses will be suspended rests with the Game Commissioner."

"It seems a pretty hard sentence for a boy as poor as Kent," April murmured.

"George Crawly and the other fellow were sentenced

194

to jail terms and fines of four hundred dollars each," Jim said drily.

Ellen shook her head sadly. "I'm sorry for Kent's parents and for Sally, but it is good to know that there will be no more shooting around here."

Jim nodded. "Deer Hill is safe now—for animals and people."

April had been too full of the jacker incident to tell her aunt of her earlier adventure with the fawn. She told the story now, while Ellen and Jim listened in amazement.

"Tomorrow morning I'll row out to the island and change the dressing on the fawn's wound," she finished. "And I hope you won't mind if I take another quart of milk, Aunt Ellen." She paused and looked at Jim in confusion. "But perhaps you won't want us using your boat now you're home, Mr. Alder."

"You will spoil my homecoming completely unless you continue to make the woods and pond entirely your own," he said quickly. "Would you like company on your row tomorrow, April? I'd enjoy meeting this wild pet of yours."

She nodded gratefully. "I'll be glad to have your company. I need help with the fawn, and I wouldn't want Kent Oliver going to the island with me again."

"April, don't be hard on Kent," Ellen protested. "He will become bitter if his friends desert him now."

195

April pressed her lips together in a tight line and stared silently at the fire.

Jim looked thoughtful. "You and young Oliver have been pretty good friends up till now, I suppose," he said to April.

"Yes—we have," she whispered, scarcely daring to speak for fear silly tears would start.

Abruptly Jim changed the subject and began to tell Ellen and April something about what the Deer Hill country had been like when he was a boy.

"My grandfather could remember Indians camping on the island where April has hidden her fawn. What tales he could tell of the Indians and the wildlife in this part of Maine."

"Do you remember the stories?" April asked eagerly.

"It is because I remember them so vividly that I decided to come home to Maine and write some of them down."

"Oh, wonderful!" cried April. "There's going to be a book about Maine forests and wildlife."

"We'll see—we'll see," he replied, his dark eyes twinkling.

April slipped around to the kitchen side of the chimney and returned in a short while with a tray of cake and steaming cups of coffee. She placed the tray on a small table in front of the fireplace and served her aunt and Mr. Alder.

"This is the greatest!" Jim Alder exclaimed, reaching

for his third chocolate cupcake. "I had almost forgotten how good homemade cake can taste. Are you the author of these cupcakes, April?"

She shook her head ruefully. "Aunt Ellen made them."

"I'm afraid you'll be seeing a lot of me from now on, Miss Merriman," Jim said with a boyish laugh. "I'll be keeping bachelor quarters in my house up the road, and somehow the prospect of eating my own cooking fails to arouse my enthusiasm."

"The latchstring is always out," she assured him. "And if it is chocolate you crave, April makes marvelous brownies."

Jim Alder rose to take his leave—all too soon for April. "I'm planning to renovate my house," he said, as he took Ellen's hand in farewell. "And perhaps stay at home for good."

As they stood together, Ellen's blue-eyed fairness was in striking contrast to his black hair and dark complexion.

"It's a lovely old place," she said. "Bringing it back to life should be a most pleasurable experience."

He looked from her to April. "There will be many points on which I'll need feminine advice. Will you both be kind enough to help me?"

Ellen looked frankly delighted. "I've been dying to get inside that darling old house ever since I first laid eyes on it. We'll be glad to help in any way we can; won't we, April?"

April nodded, but without enthusiasm.

She wondered if she would ever again be able to see the Alder place without conjuring up at the same time the picture of Kent Oliver standing shamefaced before the game warden.

After their visitor had gone, Ellen looked at her watch. "I'm afraid it is too late to call on the Olivers tonight. I'll go over in the morning, while you and Mr. Alder are visiting your fawn."

April looked relieved. "Good! I don't want to go to see the Olivers for fear of meeting Kent."

"You'll have to meet him sometime." A note of sternness rang in Ellen's pleasant voice. "If you stay away from the Olivers now, you'll hurt Sally deeply," she warned. "Sally will think you are avoiding her because her brother has been arrested."

"As though anything Kent might do could make any difference in my friendship for Sally!" April cried indignantly. "I just don't want to see Kent."

She had liked him so! And all the while he had been breaking the law and murdering deer. He was no better than George Crawly!

She ran to her room, but before she closed the door she paused with her hand still on the knob and her face turned away so her aunt could not see her tears.

Aunt Ellen was right; she mustn't take any chance of hurting Sally.

"Tell Sally I'll be over tomorrow afternoon," she said in a low voice.

If Kent Oliver had the nerve to come around where she was, she'd just treat him like a stranger.

Jim Alder failed to appear at Deer Hill Cottage the next morning, so April walked alone down the tote road, expecting to meet him at the wharf. Instead, when she reached the pond, it was lanky Kent Oliver who was standing at the end of the wharf, his hands thrust into the back pockets of his dungarees as he stared moodily across the pond.

April stopped short in confusion. She was not prepared to face Kent this morning—she needed time to decide just how to act toward him. As she stood wondering if she could slip away without him being aware of her, Kent swung around to face her. Her face turned scarlet as she remembered how quick his ears were to catch and identify every tiny sound in the woods. Of course he had known all along that she was there!

His face was stony and unfriendly.

"Mr. Alder telephoned from the inn to say he has been delayed. He asked me to row you over to the island."

"I—I can row myself."

Kent looked as if she had slapped his face.

"Okay," he said roughly. "It wasn't my idea to go. I had a suspicion I wouldn't be welcome."

April fidgeted at a knothole in the wharf with the toe

of her moccasin. Then she lifted her troubled eyes to his.

"Oh, Kent! How could you do it!"

"I suppose you are referring to the deer poaching," he said in a sarcastic tone of voice. Then suddenly his defenses crumpled. "Gosh, April," he cried impulsively. "I sure don't understand how I could have been such a fool!"

"I don't know how you could either, Kent Oliver! I bet your mother is just about sick from the shock. Why didn't you think of her and your father—and Sally!"

His mouth tightened. "I did think of them—that is, I thought I was doing it for them. But, looking back now, it seems crazy that I could have thought that money earned by poaching would ever bring us any good. I didn't even help Pop because he made me turn over to the Judge the money I earned by poaching, and now I've got to earn my fine instead of helping at home. I'm going to work for Mr. Alder," he confided. "At his house and in the woods. And, after I have paid off my fine, I'm still to have a job with him Saturdays and during vacations, whenever Pop can spare me. Since the Alder house is so near to ours, it will be easy to work on both places."

"And I suppose, in the fall, when the hunting season opens, you'll be out gunning for deer again," April said coldly.

"They may not let me have a license," Kent said in a thin voice.

April noted that his face looked less boyish and his mouth was much firmer than when she had first known him. His eyes met hers squarely. "I'll never shoot again for sport."

Her heart lifted.

"I'm so glad, Kent. Hunting is a cruel sport."

Kent shook his head. "If a man is the right sort, hunting and fishing can be eye-openers for him as to what else he can find in the woods. Mr. Alder used to be a hunter, but now, he tells me, he does his hunting with a camera. But it was hunting with a gun that got him interested in animals in the first place. I'm not condemning the chaps who hunt under the law," Kent added firmly. "But *I* won't be doing it again."

His gray eyes looked past April into the green woods. "I can understand now how Jan found the biggest thrill of all in letting the great stag go, when at last his chance had come to shoot him."

"You have really changed about hunting," April said with a little sigh of thankfulness.

"Yes." His strong hands closed gently on her arms as his gaze came back to her. "You know what changed me, April?"

She shook her head, her heart thumping.

"It was when you said that seeing the big buck killed was like witnessing a murder. There were tears in your eyes, and I could see how you detested the fellows who had shot the buck. I—I guess I want to be your kind of a

201

man. From the first time I saw you, I knew you were my girl."

"How can I be your girl?" she whispered. "We live so far apart."

"You'd be my girl if you lived on the moon."

For a thrilling moment she thought he was going to kiss her, but he only looked at her gravely with his clear, piercing eyes.

"We're still pretty young," he said, "but in a few years we'll be grown up. You'll be my girl then, the same as now, and don't you forget it."

Her eyes were as bright and beautiful as beryls above her flushed cheeks. "I won't forget, Kent—ever."

They stepped apart, feeling suddenly shy.

"We had better get over to the island," April murmured.

The fawn was watching from the long grass as they landed. He did not go to meet them, but he did not run away either. April found his milk dish and carried it to the pond to wash it. The fawn hopped after her a few steps, his soft eyes following every move she made. When she returned and filled the dish with milk, he drank greedily. Then he nibbled some cold, buttered pancakes she served on a paper plate. The coffee cake crumbs she had scattered yesterday had disappeared, but she could not guess whether the fawn or the birds were responsible.

"The little cuss seems to be much livelier today," Kent said.

April put out her hand to smooth the fawn's velvety coat. When he shied away, she looked hurt.

"Don't try to make a pet of him," Kent counseled. "Wild things are best left wild. It's good to keep the fawn on the island while he's lame, but when he's strong again the best thing would be for him to join up with a deer herd; that way he'd be with them when they yard up for the winter with the does and fawns under the protection of some big buck."

April looked at him beseechingly. "Oh, Kent, couldn't you and Sally take the fawn home and care for him when I'm gone? I would like to think of him being there with you, Pete and Tinkerbell, and—and even the earthworms."

Kent shook his head. "Pop wouldn't allow a tame deer around the farm because they are too destructive to crops. Let the fawn go back to the wild, April. That's the way nature intended it to be."

"I guess you're right, Kent," April said, after a little pause.

She sat down in the grass to watch the fawn nuzzle his pancakes.

He was the first pet she had ever had. It was hard to think that someday soon he would wander away to join the wild deer and she would never see him again, or even know what his fate might be.

"Not that you are really my pet even now," she whispered to the unheeding fawn. "A wild, beautiful thing like you could never rightly belong to anyone."

After the fawn had finished eating, they managed to capture him, but only after quite a chase. He was really much stronger than he had been the day before. Furthermore, he seemed to suspect what they wanted of him and he had no intention of letting them wash his wound again. He hopped nimbly through the grass until Kent finally caught him and carried him over to April.

This time Kent held the fawn while April removed the bandage, moistening it so it would come loose without hurting the little fellow more than was necessary.

"What do you think, Kent?" April asked, when the leg was laid bare.

"The bleeding has stopped and the wound looks clean. I don't think it needs to be bandaged again."

He let the fawn go; it hopped away and lay down at the edge of the hemlocks, and then began to lave the wound gently with its tongue.

"He's going to pull through okay," Kent said cheerfully. "The sun and wind, and his own tongue, will complete the work of healing."

14. FAWN ISLAND

JIM ALDER WAS WAITING on the wharf when the
two young people rowed back to the mainland in the
"April-May." He looked keenly at April as he helped her
out of the boat, and smiled to see her face so bright and
serene. Kent too looked much happier than when Jim
had last seen him, which was in Judge Garfield's study
the day before. It was easy to sense that the trouble between April and Kent was now a thing of the past. Jim
looked mightily pleased that this was so.

He waited beside April while Kent tied the boat up
and put the oars under the wharf.

"Some day I'd really like to go to the island with you to visit the fawn," Jim said. "Unfortunately, this morning I had important business that kept me away."

Yes, thought April, with a sudden flash of insight, business trying to patch matters up between Kent and me!

Aloud, she said, "I'll be going over there every morning until the fawn is well." She looked fondly across the water at the little green gem floating on the pond. "The island is the most beautiful of all the lovely spots I've seen at Deer Hill. It smells so sweet—and the bushes are full of the cutest little birds, always twittering and flying in and out. It's a world all by itself. Every time I go there I feel as if I wanted to stay there forever."

"I used to feel the same way about the island when I was a boy. Sometimes I'd take a blanket and sleep out there under the summer stars, so as to be early at my fishing in the morning. The best bass hole in the pond is between the island and the other shore. I guess you and Chuck have found that out, eh, Kent?"

"Yes, sir," said Kent. "We've taken some whoppers from that deep place."

As they strolled up the tote road, April between Jim and Kent, Jim told some of his plans.

His wandering years were over, he said, and now he was going to stay in Bear Paw and start writing a novel with a Maine background. He wanted to keep his woodlands exactly as they had been when he had roamed them as a boy. He hoped to buy the land along the Indian trail across the pond and add it to his large holdings on this side, the whole to be made into a wildlife sanctuary.

"And, if you want the job, Kent, you will be ranger of the entire tract."

Kent stopped walking to stare at Mr. Alder in astonishment. In her excitement over Jim's offer, April gripped Kent's arm. The three of them stood grouped in the shady, narrow tote road.

"Some of your duties would be to clear away deadfalls, chop out dead wood, cut trails, mark the different kinds of trees, and give nature talks to the school children who will be coming out here from Bear Paw and Mayville. I'll lend a hand with most of the work."

Jim's dark face looked boyish from his enthusiasm. April and Kent were listening to him enthralled.

"We'll plant wild rice to attract waterfowl. And I have another interesting project in mind. There's a little valley across the pond where there used to be a beaver dam and pond in years gone by. The game warden tells me that the beaver have long since been trapped out, but I'll import two pairs to start a new colony. Guarding them will be one of your special duties, Kent; we won't want poachers setting traps in our beaver pond."

April felt Kent's arm go tense. He was looking at Jim Alder with the oddest expression on his thin face, almost as if he were struggling to hold back tears.

"How does all this sound to you, Kent?" Jim asked.

"It sounds just great!" Kent said in a choked voice. Then he blurted out: "I can't tell you what it means to know you would trust me with a job like that after I—"

Jim's hand went to the boy's shoulder in a very warm gesture.

"I don't know where I'd find a better man. I've talked the matter over with the game warden and he heartily approves my choice of a ranger."

When they reached Deer Hill Road, Jim said he would go on to the cottage with April. His handsome green station wagon was parked beside Ellen's car.

"I thought perhaps you and your aunt might like to go through my house this morning. I'm eager to get the work of remodeling started and there are a dozen matters on which I need your advice."

During the next few weeks April and her aunt were often at the Alder place. Jim lost no time in putting a crew of carpenters, plumbers, and painters to work. Slowly the old house stirred awake after its long years of silence. Against the glistening new white paint on the house, and the fresh, bright red of the barn, even the dark, ancient spruce trees seemed to take on a livelier hue.

Jim consulted Ellen and April about the patterns of wallpaper for the various rooms and also about the material for drapes and upholstery. He discussed with them the refinishing of his antique furniture. He wanted their help in bringing back the old-fashioned flower garden that had been his mother's pride. They pored over mail-order catalogs together, and made exciting shopping trips to Lewiston and Portland.

"It's almost as much fun as if we were fixing up a house for ourselves," April told Sally.

Sally was her old gay, bouncing self these days. Kent was working every day with the men at the Alder place, earning the money to pay his fine. And Chuck Young had taken a job at the supermarket in Bear Paw for the same purpose. From somewhere Kent also snatched time to help with the work at home. He was working harder than ever before in his energetic young life, yet April had never known him to be so cheerful and lighthearted. It seemed as though a crushing weight had rolled off his shoulders once the shameful secret of his connection with the deer poachers was out in the open and behind him forever.

Time flew by so swiftly that it was a shock to April to wake up one morning in late August and realize there were but two days remaining of her vacation at Deer Hill.

How the last weeks of this wonderful summer had sped away! Already autumn was painting the maples and the cherry birch with splashes of flame and rose-wine. School would be opening in another week, and she'd be back in Hartford, comparing notes with Jean on their vacations. That would be fun of course—and she could look forward to a humming winter of work and play. What troubled her were her very slim chances of seeing Kent and Sally again in the near future—if ever. Surely Aunt Ellen would not be coming to Maine for another vacation next year.

April and Sally had invited each other to visit when the summer was over. But Sally was so poor, and was so much needed at home, that April could not picture her going off on a trip. And the same was true of Kent. As for herself, she knew Mom wouldn't want her to go away again for a long time to come.

The sun was over the hill, stealing in long fingers of gold between the trunks of the pines. April jumped out of bed. Every remaining minute at Deer Hill was a precious thing to be held fast and enjoyed to its last second!

It had been Kent's suggestion that the old cabin at the pond be repaired and made into a museum for Jim Alder's sizable collection of Maine minerals and Indian artifacts. Jim and Kent planned to rip out the bunks and build shelves all around the room. There would be a new floor, new windows, and many other improvements.

"They'll end by building an entirely new cabin from the ground up," Sally laughed.

April shook her head. "Mr. Alder wouldn't tear the cabin down—he has a sentimental feeling for it because he wrote his first book there. They're repairing it, but not really changing it, and I'm glad," she added dreamily. "I like to think of it nestled under the pines, just as it was when I first saw it."

Today Chuck Young, as well as April and Sally, had been invited to help with the work of restoring the cabin. Ellen had promised to bring them a picnic lunch at noon.

April and Kent went down to the pond ahead of the others, to row over to the island with the fawn's milk and buttered pancakes.

"What will he think the day after tomorrow, when I don't show up?" April wondered aloud sadly, as she sat opposite Kent in the "April-May."

"He's got to start being on his own sometime—and the sooner the better," Kent said practically. "Do you want him still to be hanging around, waiting for you to bring him a bowl of milk, when blizzards are whooping over the island next winter?"

"No—of course not. But you know, Kent, the fawn is the first pet I ever had, if you can call him a pet. I'll miss him, and it would be nice to think that he'll miss me a little bit too."

"He'll miss you all right, especially at first. But he'll soon get over it when he returns to the normal life of a deer. Yet—who knows?" Kent added thoughtfully. "Maybe in his deer's heart he'll keep some memory all his life of the girl who carried him out of the woods to save his life, and who fed him pancakes on Fawn Island."

"I'm going to let myself believe so anyhow," April

said with a happier look. "And now that Mr. Alder owns practically all the land on both sides of Mik-Chik Pond, my fawn has a better chance of life next fall when the hunting season opens."

As she stepped ashore from the rowboat, something occurred to April. "You called it Fawn Island just now," she said to Kent. "Is that really the name of this island?"

He finished tying the boat up and turned to her with his slow grin.

"It is now. It never did have a name before; it was just a dot on the map of Mik-Chik Pond until you brought that little critter over here to nurse him back to health. From that day on it's been Fawn Island."

"Fawn Island! It's a lovely name, Kent. I hope it sticks."

"It will," Kent said confidently. "Mr. Alder was delighted when I mentioned the name to him."

The little deer's leg was almost completely healed now. He was skittish and playful when he left his bed in the cool hemlock grove to go to meet April. He lapped his milk and ate the pancakes hungrily. Then he pushed against April, nuzzling for the salt she had learned to use as a bait to lure him close to her. She scratched his head between his erect ears, and fondly stroked his beautiful coat. Suddenly, as if his wild nature had permitted enough petting for one day, the fawn kicked up his heels and frolicked away through the grass.

He stood at the end of the island, watching with his big, sparkling brown eyes as April and Kent rowed away.

April waved good-by. "I'll see you tomorrow," she called across the water.

Jim and his four young helpers worked hard all morning, ripping up the old, rotted puncheon floor in the cabin and piling the wood on the bank of the pond to be burned after the first snowfall. Near the cabin was a pile of new pine boards that had been brought by tractor to the end of the tote road and carried from there to the cabin site by Kent and Jim.

April and Sally paused near the wood heap to rest from their strenuous labors. At the edge of the woods tall spikes of scarlet flowers made a gaudy splash of color against the deep green of the conifers.

"Cardinal lobelia," Jim said, in answer to April's question about the red flowers. "Have you ever noticed," he added, "how nature colors her flowers to match the seasons? In spring she gives us shy hues of arbutus and hepatica, then in June come the deepening tones of pink lady slipper and columbine. And the flaunting colors of lobelia, Oswego tea, and purple asters bring in the fall."

"Why not have a wild flower garden around the Indian Museum?" April suggested. "There must be a sufficient variety of wild flowers to keep some plant in bloom from spring till snow."

Jim was delighted. "A splendid idea! We'll plant violets on the bank of the pond, mints on the beach, columbine among the rocks over there—"

"Maine's state flower is the pine cone and tassel; we surely have plenty of those for a background," said Sally. "And there's a raft of trailing arbutus on the knoll behind our pasture; we could move some of the plants down here."

"We'll try to have every plant native to our Maine woodlands growing here," Jim said with rising enthusiasm.

April listened to them wistfully. How she wished she could stay at Deer Hill to help them plant the wild flower garden! And next spring, when it started to bloom, she'd see it only through Sally's letters.

Even the boys were interested in the garden scheme and promised to help with the moving and planting.

"Don't forget to include ferns," said Kent. "To my mind a bed of ferns is the prettiest thing in the woods."

"Except partridge vines and wintergreen with their red berries gleaming under the snow," Sally reminded him.

At noon Jim walked up the trail to meet Ellen. Soon thereafter they returned to the cabin pulling Sally's travois between them. The travois was loaded with an earthenware pot full of bubbling baked beans, a basket of fried chicken, crusty rolls, a bowl of potato salad garnished with lettuce and tomatoes, and a lucious chocolate cake. There was also a gallon jug of hot coffee, and ice cream neatly packed in dry ice—this last being Jim's contribution.

"Work's over for today, gang!" Jim shouted. "It's picnic time and play time from now on."

It was a gay picnic they had under the pines. Jim sat close to Ellen, and once April saw his hand steal out and clasp hers in the wide folds of her circle skirt. Ellen turned her head to smile at him with a new luster in her blue eyes. The glance they exchanged was as thrilling as a kiss. April glanced quickly away with a tingling feeling that she had stumbled on something infinitely lovely.

"There's romance in the air," Kent whispered with his lips close to her ear.

Jim and Ellen fell into a deep discussion of Jim's new book. Sally and Chuck were fishing with drop lines off the big rock, laughing and joshing as they always did when they were together.

Kent stood up and pulled April to her feet. They wandered off along the trail to the wharf.

Now, at the end of summer, the sky was a deeper blue and the sunshine had never been so golden. Great masses of clouds, cotton-white and rimmed with silver, towered in the vast reaches of the sky.

"What a lovely day," April murmured. "A day to remember till summer comes again. I start back tomorrow at noon," she added with a sigh.

"You won't forget what I told you at the wharf that

day, when you're back with all those sleek fellows at Hartford High?" asked Kent.

April laughed. "They're not so sleek, Kent. You and my friends and my brother Perry would hit it off fine." Her face sobered. "No, I'll never forget. But I'd like to hear you say it again," she said softly.

Hands clasped, they stood facing each other in the lacy shade of the pines and hemlocks.

"You're my girl," said Kent. "And don't you ever forget it!"

He bent his head and kissed her cheek at the corner of her mouth. Then, as they heard Sally and Chuck coming along the trail, they walked on slowly. Under her breath, just loud enough for Kent to hear, April repeated Jan's verse from the *Trail of the Sandhill Stag*.

These are the best days of my life.
These are my golden days—

That night, when the three of them were alone at Deer Hill Cottage, Ellen and Jim told April that they were engaged to be married. At first April was stunned by the suddenness with which this state of affairs had come about, but then she told herself that anyone with a grain of sense would have guessed all along that Ellen and Jim were falling in love.

After Jim had gone back to Bear Paw, April kissed her aunt and once again wished her happiness.

"Mom and Daddy are going to be happy for you, too, when they hear about you and Mr. Alder."

Ellen nodded. There was a sparkling glow on her lovely face tonight.

"I never expected to fall in love again," she confessed.

Her face sobered a little and her blue eyes grew pensive as she looked at the magnificent new diamond glittering on her left hand.

"I was attracted to Jim the very first time I saw him," she said softly after a moment.

She began to tell April about the plans they had made for the wedding. If April's parents were agreeable, and both Ellen and April were sure that they would be, the wedding would take place at the Merriman home on Thanksgiving Day. April was delighted to learn that Jim planned to bring both Sally and Kent to Hartford with him. April was to be her aunt's bridesmaid, and Kent would be Jim's best man.

As April discussed all this with Ellen, a happy thought blossomed in her mind. Now she would be able to spend part of every vacation at the Alder place near Sally and Kent. She could hardly wait to tell them!

To her aunt, she said: "When we were helping Mr. Alder fix up his house, did you know it was to be your own home in the future?"

Ellen laughed. "I guess I had a sort of feeling about it. Anyhow, if you ever want to see my dream house come to life, just walk down the road and look at the Alder place."

"It's hard to believe that Jim Alder is going to be one of our family," mused April. "I certainly never dreamed of such a thing when I was reading his book last winter."

"Nor I," Ellen smiled.

Suddenly April slapped the arm of her chair with her fist. "Am I dumb!" she cried. "I know now why Mr. Alder always looked so familiar to me when I met him at the pond—of course I had seen his picture loads of times on the jackets of his books."

"Of course," Ellen agreed. "I recognized him the first time I saw him, even before he introduced himself."

It was Jim who rowed April out to the island the following morning.

"Kent had some work to do for his father this morning," he explained. "He asked me to tell you he would be at the station to see you off and to say good-by until Thanksgiving."

April hid her disappointment. Much as she liked Jim Alder, it was Kent's company she longed for on this last trip to Fawn Island.

The island seemed strangely still and lonely when they reached it. There was no sound of birds in the thickets, and, for the first time in weeks, the fawn failed to be on hand to greet April. April and Jim searched the hemlock grove and looked into every possible place of concealment on the little island. Finally they had to admit that the fawn just wasn't there.

"He saw some other deer, probably a doe and a fawn, swimming the pond, and he took off after them," Jim guessed. "It's the best thing for him," he added gently, "to go home to the forest and the deer people."

April nodded. But there was a lump in her throat and tears in her eyes as she looked across the water to the Indian oak.

Don't wander far, my fawn, she prayed. Stay in Jim Alder's sheltering woods where you'll be safe forever from guns and hunters.

Jim put a comforting arm about her shoulders. From his pocket he took an official-looking document and handed it to her.

"This is my wedding present to you, April."

A laugh sparkled through her tears.

"I'm not the one who's getting married."

"It's your wedding present just the same, from your Uncle Jim."

With eager interest she unfolded the heavy paper. It was a deed in her name to Fawn Island in Mik-Chik Pond.

"The ground you are standing on belongs to you now," Jim told her. "A little bit of the state of Maine to call you back here every year."

April, holding the deed to her island tight against her heart, promised the blue pond and the murmuring pines that never would a year go by when she failed to heed the call.